"Why didn't you tell me to go?"

Brandt demanded quietly. "I thought you were different." The lack of anger in his voice made his words all the more cutting. "But you're as self-centered as the rest."

The acid sting of tears burned Joan's eyes as she forced out the words. "And how does a person go about ordering her boss to leave—without losing her job!"

Her heart was shattering into a thousand pieces like splintering glass, knowing he believed she had deceived him. Suddenly Brandt turned her around and his mouth punishingly covered hers for a white-hot moment.

When he released her, his eyes were cutting her to the quick. "Tell me, Joan, were you really afraid of losing your job...or did you see a means of keeping it...?"

JANET DAILEY AMERICANA

Every novel in this collection is your passport to a romantic tour of the United States through time-honored favorites by America's First Lady of romance fiction. Each of the fifty novels is set in a different state, researched by Janet and her husband, Bill. For the Daileys it was an odyssey of discovery. For you, it's the journey of a lifetime.

The state flower depicted on the cover of this book is native violet.

Janet Dailey Americana
ALABAMA—Dangerous Masquerade
ALASKA—Northern Magic
ARIZONA—Sonora Sundown
ARKANSAS—Valley of the Vapours
CALIFORNIA—Fire and Ice
COLORADO—After the Storm
CONNECTICUT—Difficult Decision
DELAWARE—The Matchmakers
FLORIDA—Southern Nights
GEORGIA—Night of the Cotillion
HAWAII—Kona Winds
IDAHO—The Travelling Kind
ILLINOIS—A Lyon's Share
INDIANA—The Indy Man

Don't miss any of our special offers. Write to us at the following address for information on our newest releases.

Harlequin Reader Service
901 Fuhrmann Blvd., P.O. Box 1397, Buffalo, NY 14240
Canadian address: P.O. Box 603,
Fort Erie, Ont. L2A 5X3

A LYON'S SHARE

Harlequin Books

TORONTO • NEW YORK • LONDON
AMSTERDAM • PARIS • SYDNEY • HAMBURG
STOCKHOLM • ATHENS • TOKYO • MILAN

Janet Dailey Americana edition published December 1986
ISBN 373-89813-4

Harlequin Presents edition published October 1977
Second printing March 1980
Third printing April 1981

Original hardcover edition published in 1976
by Mills & Boon Limited

CHAPTER ONE

'FOR heaven's sake, Joan! Stop being an old stick in the mud!' Kay sighed impatiently. 'Name me one thing you have planned to do tonight that can't be put off until tomorrow.'

Joan Somers refused to meet her room-mate's accusing gaze as she gathered the wrappings from her sandwich and the empty milk carton on to the canteen tray.

'That isn't the point. You know how I feel about blind dates,' Joan stated.

'Ed can hardly be classified as a blind date. He's John's brother,' Kay argued.

John Turner was Kay's fiancé, a likeable man, but in Joan's opinion, dull and unexciting. His one endearing quality was his devotion to Kay, a love that he managed to show in a hundred different romantic ways. Still, it was unlikely that Joan would find his brother's company any more stimulating than she found John's. He simply wasn't her type, although at twenty-three she was beginning to wonder if she had a type.

'Why don't you ask Susan instead?' Joan suggested, referring to the girl that operated the switchboard.

There was a derisive roundness to Kay's sparkling brown eyes. 'Have you ever known Susan to have a free hour on the weekends? That girl has more men around her than a bunch of nude bathing beauties,' her room-mate replied scornfully. 'She'd never have a Friday night open.'

'That's true,' Joan agreed. A twinge of self-pity reminded her that she was the only one who seemed to spend most of her weekends in her apartment—alone.

'You simply have to go tonight,' Kay pleaded. 'John only found out this morning that Ed was flying in to meet me. There isn't anyone else I can get on such short notice.'

'He's coming in to meet *you*,' Joan emphasised. 'Why don't the three of you just go somewhere for dinner?'

'Ed is John's brother, not his uncle!' Kay declared, rising to her feet and following Joan as she left the table.

Joan glanced at her watch. 'Let's discuss it after work tonight,' she stalled. 'I have to get back to the office.'

'I can't wait until five o'clock.' Her room-mate ignored the hallway that branched to their right, the hallway that led to the computer department where Kay worked, and followed Joan into the sector of the private offices of Lyon Construction. 'John is picking me up after work and we're going straight to O'Hare Field to meet Ed when he gets off his plane. I have to know now.'

Joan was backed into a corner and she knew it. Even as she held back her agreement, she knew she was going to give in to her friend's persuasions. She had no valid reason not to agree. Joan prided herself on being practical and logical, which made her superstitious avoidance of blind dates seem childishly silly.

Simply because she had met Rick Manville on a blind date four years ago and had fallen victim to his charm only to discover there were many other victims to keep her company, there was not any reason to think she would make a fool of herself again. There had been more humiliation than hurt when she had realised she was just another girl to him. Looking back she could see how very callow he had been, but at the time, Rick had seemed manly and strong. It had taken a truly strong and self-assured man to make her see that, though.

'Joan, you simply have to come tonight,' Kay insisted again in a pleading tone. 'John and I are counting on you.'

Her gaze studied the cocker spaniel look of the pert brunette beside her as Joan paused at the outer office door. In so many ways, she and Kay were such opposites. Kay, with her dark pixie curls, was slight, petitely built, bubbling with an outgoing personality while Joan was statuesque and full-figured, her long amber hair coiled in a practical bun on the back of her neck. Her eyes were a warm brown but without that special sparkle of Kay's. Her attitude was as friendly as her room-mate's, but quieter and less obtrusive. It was difficult for Joan to meet strangers on a social basis, especially men. Kay would enter into a project with madcap abandon while Joan would efficiently organise each step.

7

Instead of trying to find a way out of the blind date, Joan knew she should be leaping at the opportunity to have a night out. Too many weekends she had spent alone lately. Still, it was difficult to force the words of agreement through her lips. She pushed open the door to her office and walked in, with Kay on her heels.

'You can't let us down,' Kay repeated. 'We want to——'

The rest of her sentence was lost as she caught sight of the man standing beside the open drawer of the filing cabinet. Kay's face was immediately wreathed with a bright smile.

'Good afternoon, Mr Lyon.'

But her cheery greeting didn't alter the rugged planes of his face as he nodded curtly in Kay's direction before his sharp blue gaze swung to Joan. There was an aura of boundless energy and an unshakeable stamp of command and competence, simultaneously unnerving and reassuring.

'Miss Somers, will you please tell me where in this mess I might find the Statler file?' His fingers raked the thick brown mane of his hair before his hand returned to his hip in a challenging position.

The criticism, completely unwarranted, raised Joan's chin a fraction of an inch in defiance. She walked crisply to the metal cabinet where he was standing.

'Perhaps, Mr Lyon, if you would stay out of the files, they wouldn't be in such a mess,' she replied, and began reinserting the partially removed folders. 'In the first place, the Statler file wouldn't be in this drawer since this is strictly material suppliers.'

With the drawer in reasonable order again, she closed it and pulled open the one beneath it, aware of the tall, broad-shouldered figure towering at her side. At the rear of the alphabetical index under 'S', her fingers fumbled through the folders, the smaller letters of the name tabs blurring before her eyes.

'What's the matter, Miss Somers?' Her employer's wry voice sounded above her head. 'Can't you find it either?'

'Yes, I can find it.' Joan stiffly straightened and walked to her desk.

Her tortoiseshell glasses of amber and brown were lying beside the telephone. She had often laughed that she could see a country mile, but not an inch in front of her nose. At this moment, she didn't find her dependence on glasses for reading at all humorous.

'But I, unfortunately, can't read the name tabs without my glasses,' she stated as she slipped on the glasses and walked back to the cabinet.

In the span of a few seconds, she was handing him the folder he had requested. The aquiline features were turned towards the folder so Brandt Lyon missed her prim smile of victory.

'Some day, Miss Somers,' her employer spoke absently as he started towards his private office, 'you are going to have to draw me a set of blueprints so I can find things in that metal monster of yours.'

Her lips were pressed tightly together as the door

to his connecting office closed behind him. His criticism had been uttered in a moment of exasperation and had not been meant as a slight to her ability. Still, the barbs did prick.

'You amaze me sometimes, Joan.' Kay shook her head wryly.

'Why?' Joan walked around the desk to her chair and slipped her bag into the bottom drawer of her desk.

'Talking back to Mr Lyon the way you just did. Imagine telling the boss to stay out of his own files!' she laughed. 'No wonder you two don't get along.'

'Mr Lyon and I get along very well,' Joan said stiffly.

'What I mean is you're hardly friendly. Everything is strictly business. For all the notice he pays you, you could be a fifty-year-old grandmother. And you're just as bad. You act as if he's fifty instead of a very eligible bachelor.'

'I'm his secretary, not his mistress.'

'Well,' Kay sighed, 'you'll never be his mistress if you keep calling him Mr Lyon all the time.'

'That's what you called him,' Joan pointed out.

'Yes, but look how seldom I see him. If I were his secretary, I sure would be making a play for him.'

'And probably end up losing a well-paying job. Besides,' Joan teased, slipping her glasses off, 'what would John think if he knew you had eyes for the president of the company?'

'He would be jealous, wouldn't he?' Kay giggled. 'But he knows I'm a big flirt.'

'I sometimes think that's an understatement,' Joan smiled ruefully.

'Speaking of John, what about tonight?'

The corners of her mouth turned abruptly down. 'I'll go,' she agreed with a resigned nod. 'But I won't entertain John's brother the entire weekend. It will only be for tonight.'

'Thanks loads!' Kay breathed. 'We're coming straight to the apartment from the airport. We ought to be there around seven-thirty, so be ready when we get there.'

'I will.'

The intercom buzzer sounded. 'Yes?' Joan answered.

'Will you come into my office, Miss Somers?' Brandt Lyon's voice responded.

Kay was halfway to the door to leave when she turned around to add a parting remark. 'And wear something sexy, too!'

For a split second, Joan could only stare at the button she had pushed, holding her breath in hopes that her room-mate's words had not been picked up by the intercom speaker.

'I'll be right there, Mr Lyon,' she murmured.

Breaking off the connection, she slipped her glasses back on and gathered her pencil and paper. At the door to his office, she paused to straighten the tweed skirt of her tailored suit, then walked in.

The big leather chair swung around as she entered. The perusal of his gaze was very thorough as it swept over her. Joan guessed what he was thinking, knowing how deceptive the severe hair-style and tortoiseshell glasses were. Brandt Lyon was undoubtedly questioning her ability to appear sexy.

Then a shutter closed, blanking out the gleam of speculation, and his look was no longer personal but strictly business, employer to employee. With an efficiency that matched Joan's, he went through his schedule for the afternoon, handed her the cartridges from his dictaphone containing the morning's dictation, and added a list of telephone calls he wanted her to make.

The impersonal business level had been re-established. No reference was made to confirm or deny that he had overheard Kay's comment. That swift appraisal of her when she had walked in the door might never have occurred.

Yet at five o'clock, Joan stepped into the doorway of his office to make certain there was nothing else he required of her before she left for the weekend. His casual remark stripped the doubt that remained.

'Are you going out this evening, Miss Somers?' Brandt Lyon inquired after assuring her there was nothing else he needed.

'It's Friday,' she replied, trying to make it sound as if it was customary for her to have a date instead of a rarity.

'Enjoy yourself.'

There was no mockery in his statement, nor any teasing barb, but she took exception to his indifferent wish. 'I generally do, Mr Lyon. Goodnight.'

The wind had a bite of the cold north in its teeth as Joan waited on the corner for her bus. The late

November snowfall had melted, leaving the ground frozen and barren on the first days of December. Dusk was encroaching on the grey skies, but the heavy overcast didn't permit the golden pink colours of sunset to peep through the clouds.

The weekends were generally quiet respites from work, punctuated by evenings with girl friends or the occasional date. In the rush of the Chicago traffic, Joan felt gloomy and lost. She knew the cause – that last indifferent comment from Brandt Lyon.

When she had graduated from the secretarial college, she had worked in a typing pool at a large insurance firm for nine months. Then she had seen the advertisement in the newspaper for a private secretary. On that day three years ago, she had gone to Lyon Construction to fill out her application. There she had met Kay Moreland who was there in answer to another advertisement for a vacancy in the computer section.

Two days later she had received a call to come for an interview. Brandt Lyon had been rummaging through the file cabinet looking for a folder that day, too. He hadn't wasted time with introductions as he had told her what he was looking for and asked her to find it. It had taken her only a few minutes to work out the system and produce the required folder.

By that time Brandt Lyon was talking to someone on a long-distance phone call. He held the call long enough to thank her and to ask her to make coffee. When that task had been completed, Joan had waited nervously in the outer office, a little stunned to find her prospective employer so young, or at least relatively young, since he had been in his early thirties. There had been such a positive air about him, a sense that he always got things done one way or another, that Joan had found herself smiling when she remembered that look of exasperation on his rugged face when he hadn't been able to find the folder he wanted from the cabinet.

At about that moment, he had stepped into the office. She had been uncomfortably conscious of the appraisal in his dark blue eyes and had wondered if he was the type that constantly chased his secretary around the desk. She had even speculated that it might be exciting to be caught.

'I had wanted someone older with more experience,' he had said.

Joan remembered the way her heart had quickened at the sound of his quietly spoken but firm words. His voice was one that people listened to and automatically sat straighter without realising it.

'I feel I am very well qualified for the position, Mr Lyon,' Joan had replied in her best professional voice.

'We'll see how you do,' he had nodded, and turned away.

'Do you mean I have the job?' She had been so positive he was going to turn her down that she hadn't been certain that she had interpreted his statement correctly.

'You did apply for it, didn't you?' Brandt Lyon had answered with marked patience. Joan had moved her head in an affirmative gesture. 'Well, you've got it, starting right now.'

In the beginning, she had assumed that he had made a snap decision based on his need for an immediate replacement for her predecessor, who had been badly injured in an automobile accident. Gradually Joan learned via the office grapevine that he had investigated her background thoroughly before calling her in for the interview. Still, she secretly believed that her ability to fathom the filing system instantly had been the key to her hiring.

Kay had been hired only the day before and as the two latest additions to the Lyon staff, they gravitated towards each other despite the differences in their respective positions. Within a few months, they were sharing an apartment.

Joan readily admitted to herself that in the first few months in her new job she had developed a crush on her boss. Brandt Lyon was a dynamic individual. Rarely had Joan ever seen him ruffled by anything. Whatever obstacle or crisis that occurred was met calmly and solved, or removed from his path. His surname conjured up the image of a jungle cat and he was very much like the lion. His strength and power were only hinted at, roused only when there was need and not in anger. His ruggedness, the features that weren't handsome but compelling, increased the comparison.

Yes, she had nourished secret hopes in the beginning that he might look at her as a woman, but it had always been business. Joan herself had set the foundations for their relationship. She had been overly conscious of her youth, in his eyes, and had done her utmost to play it down. When she had started the job, her wardrobe had consisted of sweaters and skirts. Gradually she had revamped it into tailored suits, attractive but hardly eye-catching.

Her long amber-golden hair was no longer caught by a scarf at the back of her neck, but coiled into a severe style that darkened its shimmering colour. The necessity for glasses merely completed the picture of a prim, professional secretary. Awareness that she was attracted to him made Joan all the more conscious of the way she addressed him for fear he might guess.

It was true that nearly all the employees were on a first-name basis with their respective department heads. Even the engineers and project superintendents referred to Brandt Lyon by his first name. But Joan had been afraid that someone might discover her hidden crush if she became too familiar and friendly with her boss.

A secret love can only be cherished for so long before it becomes inevitable that it must die from lack of nourishment. Brandt Lyon's total lack of interest in her life outside of the office and her duties made the death come more swiftly. Joan was grateful that the practical side of her nature had never allowed her to confide her secret feelings to anyone. Not even her room-mate guessed how close her teasing remarks had come to the truth.

Admiration and respect were the only emotions

that Joan allowed to exist for her employer now. Yet she knew she was still overly sensitive to his indifference. There was a part of her that wanted him to see her as a woman and not a faithful secretary capable of fathoming a filing system he found impossible.

The bus stopped at her corner and Joan pushed her way through the passengers to the side door. The wind chased her to the apartment building, its cold breath trying to penetrate the scarf around her neck. Inside the building she bypassed the elevators for the stairs leading to the second floor and the apartment she shared with Kay.

Kay liked to describe the decor as 'early left-overs' since the two-room apartment had been furnished with items neither of their parents wanted any more. It was a genuine hodge-podge of styles ranging from a heavy Mediterranean-style sofa to an Early American rocker. A sink unit occupied one corner of the front room. A white stove and a copper-coloured refrigerator added to the incongruity of the apartment.

The second room of their apartment was the bedroom, with twin beds and a small adjoining bathroom. Joan removed her heavy winter coat and pushed it into the crowded wardrobe, then slipped off the jacket of her suit and tossed it on the rose-coloured chenille bedspread.

She traipsed half-heartedly back to the kitchen area, trying to summon enthusiasm for the coming evening and her date with John's brother as she fixed a half-pot of coffee. Even though she knew she had got over her crush on Brandt Lyon, Joan knew she would compare Ed Thomas with him. In three years, she hadn't met any man in Brandt Lyon's class.

Not that she had dated often enough to compare him with many men. Joan had never been much of a social person, even in high school. She had generally been too tall for most of the boys her age. Once she was out of school, she discovered it wasn't as easy as she had thought it would be to meet single men. She wasn't comfortable going to night clubs in the company of other girls in hopes of meeting a new eligible face, which was the reason she spent most of her evenings alone in her apartment.

At the office, ninety per cent of the males were married and the other ten per cent Joan didn't care about. Besides, she had discovered that her position as Brandt Lyon's secretary was something of a handicap. She was either pursued or avoided because of her closeness to the head of the firm.

Joan glanced longingly at the half-finished book lying on the table beside the sofa, knowing she didn't dare pick it up or else she would become so engrossed in it that she would lose all track of time and not be ready when Kay returned. She had so looked forward to reading the rest of that book tonight, she sighed, then laughed. The sound of her laughter echoed in the room.

'That's a fine state of affairs,' Joan chided herself aloud, 'when I find reading a novel more enjoyable than my love life!'

Resolutely she walked into the bathroom and turned on the water taps to the tub, pouring a liberal amount of bubble bath in the bottom. Searching through her closet, she found the coffee silk trouser suit and laid it out on the bed, removing the gold metal belt from her jewel case. Wear something sexy, Kay had decreed, and Joan was going to do her best to fulfil the order.

The coffee pot stopped perking a few minutes after she was through with her bath. Sitting on the blue velvet sofa with her coffee cup on the scarred table, Joan began removing the pins from the coiled knot of her hair. It shimmered like molten gold over her shoulders, the overhead light picking out the sunny highlights. Vigorously she brushed it until it crackled and snapped.

Her father had once said the length of her hair was the only unpractical thing about Joan. With her hair down and curling about her shoulders, she always felt so feminine. A shorter hairstyle would have been a great deal more practical, but she had never summoned the nerve to have it cut off. Only long did the natural brassy shade of her hair look right.

When Kay, John, and his brother arrived, Joan was glad she had taken extra time with her appearance. Even John, accustomed to seeing her in denims and sweaters, looked twice. The coffee brown trouser suit accented the gold of her hair and the velvet shade of brown in her eyes. The clinging silk moulded her full figure and the slender curves of her legs.

19

'Kay, you never told me your room-mate was a blonde.' Ed Thomas was holding her hand, his hazel eyes roaming freely over Joan's face.

In looks, he resembled John, a couple of inches taller perhaps, but the same light brown shade of hair and similar bone structure. Yet John's face always gave the impression of gentle understanding and Ed's expression had a raffish air. Joan wasn't sure she liked that gleam in his eyes either. Then she immediately scolded herself for being so prudish.

Since meeting Rick Manville, the wolf-type made her cautious. Their open admiration and profuse compliments usually were made to breach a girl's defences. Joan managed a smile and pulled her hand free of his hold.

'Did you have a good flight ... Ed?' she faltered slightly over his name as she took the white fun-fur coat that Kay handed her.

'It was on time, which in this day and age makes it an excellent flight,' he joked, quickly taking the initiative to help her with the coat. Once the fur material was around her shoulders, Ed Thomas squeezed them gently and winked. 'I had John make reservations for the best eating place around. We might have more to celebrate than their engagement.'

'We'd better be going before we're late,' John spoke, but it was more of a suggestion than a statement. 'Pierre's won't hold your reservation if you're not on time.'

Naturally John drove since he was the one familiar with the area and Kay sat in the front seat with him, which left Joan in back alone with Ed. She discovered there wasn't any need for small talk, at least on her part, since he was very willing to carry the conversation. He wasn't a bit boring, she decided as she remembered the uncomfortable silences that descended with most of her dates. He had the same facility to put her at her ease as Rick Manville had, but she had gained sufficient experience from Rick not to be swayed by Ed's undivided attention.

At the dinner table, Ed was even able to draw out long sentences from his brother John, who was generally less talkative. He had both Kay and Joan laughing with anecdotes of their childhood. From the restaurant, the two couples migrated to the lounge area where the mood was more intimate and the conversation was less boisterous.

It was nearly midnight when John suggested that they leave. Joan was smiling contentedly, unable to remember when she had enjoyed an evening so much. She still didn't altogether trust the flirtatious escort, but her ego had sublimely enjoyed being the centre of his attention.

Only when they had risen from their table did Joan notice the couple on the small dance floor. The fragile blonde in a cloud of pink caught her eye first, being the epitome of everything dainty and feminine that Joan had wanted to be. Then she noticed the man holding her in his arms. It was Brandt Lyon, the masculine line of his mouth curved into a smile.

Her stomach turned over with sickening suddenness. She had always known there were other women in his life. With a man like Brandt Lyon, there were bound to be. On odd occasions, she had even taken messages over the telephone that would confirm it, but she had never seen him in the company of a woman.

At that moment the woman snuggled her head against his chest. Joan watched his gaze lazily sweep the room while he made some whispered comment to his partner. For a fraction of a second, his gaze lingered on her. She waited in breathless anticipation for his nod of recognition before his attention reverted to his partner.

Her teeth bit into her lips as she realised with a start that her boss hadn't recognised her. A wistful smile curled her lips as she wondered what his reaction would be if she identified herself to him. Would he revise his opinion about his efficient secretary or would he still doubt her ability to be attractive?

Then Ed's arm was curling around her shoulders, urging her towards the door. His touch took her out of the world of makebelieve and into reality. Her crush on Brandt Lyon had been over a long time ago. She had to end this foolish speculation. The truth was that even if he did suddenly see her as a woman, she could never compete with the likes of the blonde in his arms.

It was a waste of time to keep pining for someone who was out of her reach. Joan pushed aside the romantic dreamings and called upon the stronger, practical side of her nature. Ed Thomas was nice, much nicer than she expected. It was time she stopped comparing each man she met with Brandt Lyon. Men were individuals and she had to begin looking at them as such and stop trying to put them into categories.

Infatuations were all right when she was young. Now she was older, supposed to be wiser.

CHAPTER TWO

KAY teased Joan unmercifully about her vow that she wouldn't entertain Ed the entire weekend. In fact, Joan had ended up going to the airport to see him off that Sunday. She decided that she had needed to see Brandt Lyon with another woman to completely kill the last of her infatuation. And Ed had been all too willing to fill the gap, not in any serious way, however.

Joan still believed he was something of a playboy, but she truly hadn't minded. Although she had to admit she was rather surprised by the flowers he had sent to her the day after he left and the telephone call from Cleveland on Wednesday. He had even made plans to fly back to Chicago the weekend before Christmas. It was obvious she had impressed him, and that filled her with confidence.

Outside her office window, flakes of snow were swirling in a light wind. The weekend promised to be white and Joan began to daydream about her plans for the following day. She and Kay were going shopping for the remainder of their Christmas gifts. She wondered if she should buy some small gift for Ed, nothing expensive or personal, but a little something.

The intercom buzzed commandingly. 'Miss

Somers,' Brandt Lyon's voice sounded crisply over the speaker. 'bring me in those figures Jenson left with you on the Danville hospital.'

'Yes. sir,' Joan responded promptly, flicking off the intercom switch as she rose from her desk.

She was nearly to the filing cabinets when the buzz of the intercom called her back. 'Get Lyle Baines in here. The figures on this hospital bid don't look right. I want to go over them with him before we submit it.'

The idle moments of the first hour of the morning disappeared as Joan found herself running back and forth from the filing cabinet to Brandt Lyon's office. An error was found in the computations for the hospital construction bid and now every item was being double checked.

At noon, Kay stuck her head inside the door asking Joan if she was going to lunch. Joan glanced towards the closed door and grimaced.

'I doubt if they know what time it is. Bring me back a sandwich,' she asked her room-mate.

'I bet they haven't looked outside either,' Kay smiled. 'It's turning into a regular blizzard. You'd better put a bird on the boss's shoulder so someone will tell him that he'd better let us go home early.' With a cheery wave. Kay closed the door.

Joan looked out the window. The gentle snowfall had turned into a solid curtain of wind-driven snow. The practical side refused to leap to conclusions as she picked up the telephone and dialled the weather bureau. Heavy snowfall and blizzard conditions were forecast. Another telephone call confirmed that some of the side streets were becoming impassable and the city government was recommending that those businesses that could close early, should.

Rapping once on the inner office door, Joan entered the private office. Brandt Lyon was bent over his desk, his brown suitcoat thrown across a side chair, his tie loosened. The top buttons of his white shirt were unbuttoned and the cuffs of his long sleeves were rolled back. The fingers of one hand continued their race over the keys of the portable calculator while he ambidextrously entered the results with his left hand.

'What is it, Miss Somers?' The leonine head didn't look up as he made his inquiry.

'I'm afraid we're in the middle of a blizzard, sir. They're recommending that all non-essential businesses close,' Joan replied.

The burly figure of Lyle Baines was sitting at the small draughting table in front of the window. His head raised at Joan's words to look outside.

'Hell!' he exclaimed as he stared at the snowstorm beyond the window panes. Immediately the older man glanced at Joan. 'Sorry. I forgot there was a lady around,' he apologised then sighed heavily. 'It's a first class snowstorm, Brandt. Hope this isn't a sign of what the rest of the winter is going to be like.'

Brandt Lyon swivelled his chair towards the window to confirm their statements for himself. A furrow of concentration lined his wide forehead. Broken by a wayward strand of teak brown hair.

'Some of the side streets are already becoming impassable,' Joan added quietly.

The strong fingers of one hand rubbed his chin and mouth as Brandt turned back to her. The blue of his eyes was intensified by the thickness of his brown lashes and the dark remains of his summer tan. Joan was drawn again by the strength and competency etched in the irregular features.

'Send everyone home, Miss Somers,' he ordered calmly. The brown column of his neck turned his attention to the man at the draughting table. 'We should be finished in another hour or so, Lyle.'

'There's no reason for me to rush home,' the man shrugged. 'My wife's in Peoria with our daughter.' Then he smiled proudly. 'Our first grandchild arrived on the scene—a boy. I was going to drive there after work tonight, but that's out now, thanks to the snow.'

Brandt smiled in sympathy, then raised a questioning brow at Joan. 'You'll notify everyone?'

'Right away,' she nodded, and turned to leave.

'Miss Somers,' he called her back. One corner of his mouth was lifted in rueful apology. 'I'm afraid I'll have to ask you to stay. I'll need you to retype this bid when we're done and to supply me with some more folders from your personal puzzle cabinet in the meantime.'

Joan glanced out of the window, silently wondering how long the buses could keep running in this storm. 'Of course I'll stay.' It was unthinkable to refuse.

'You go home by bus, don't you?' Brandt asked, perceptively guessing the direction of her thoughts.

'Yes.'

'Don't worry about getting home. I'll give you a

ride when we're through,' he stated, and leaned forward to resume his work.

Knowing there was nothing more behind his offer than thoughtful consideration, Joan nodded her thanks and left the room, glad that she was over her ridiculous infatuation and was beyond the time when she would have built up futile hopes at the thought of Brandt Lyon taking her home.

The building emptied quickly as the word spread that everyone was to leave. At one-thirty, Brandt sent Lyle Baines home, but it was going on three o'clock by the time Joan finished typing the corrected construction bid. While she covered the typewriter and straightened her desk, he affixed his signature and slipped the quotation into its envelope.

'It's worse, isn't it?' she murmured as she saw Brandt staring out the window.

Over his shoulder, he watched her tie the scarf around her neck, his expression grimly serious, but he gave no response to her question. His silence was a louder answer. Yet his dark vitality reassured her in some mysterious way.

Walking swiftly, they covered the distance of the corridors from his private office to the front door. The blast of wind nearly knocked Joan off her feet as they stepped outside. His arm circled her waist in support and guided her in the direction of the adjacent parking lot. Visibility had been reduced by the driving snow to only a few feet and Joan knew Brandt was guiding her to his car on instinct alone.

'This is ridiculous!' he snapped suddenly, and stopped.

In the span of a few seconds, he had turned her around and was leading her back to the building. Her teeth were already chattering from the sub-zero temperature when the door closed behind them. Almost unwillingly, she met his penetrating gaze.

'We're better off staying here,' he said, 'than taking the risk of being stranded in the car. At least, here we have food, heat and lights.'

His eyes held hers for an instant longer before Joan broke away in self-conscious confusion. The weather forecast had stated that the blizzard would continue through the night and into Saturday, which meant she and Brandt would be together for the next twenty-four hours or more.

'Of course you're right.' Logic made her agree as she busied her suddenly unsteady fingers with the knot of her scarf. 'Although once you've dined on the canteen fare, you may question whether it's food!'

'Nothing seems to shatter your poise, Miss Somers,' he grinned crookedly, 'not even the prospect of possibly being stranded for the weekend with your boss.'

Joan had seen his face transformed by a smile before, but rarely had she ever been the recipient. Quicksilver excitement danced in her veins, but she quickly drowned it with the sobering memory of the petite blonde. She couldn't admit that she wasn't looking forward to his exclusive company for the weekend. Admiration and respect were the only feelings she wanted to have towards him. To know him as more than her employer might not be safe for her carefully preserved peace of mind.

'Neither one of us is responsible for the storm,' Joan shrugged, knowing her composure at that moment was not what she would have desired it to be. A thousand inner apprehensions were hammering at her nerves. 'It doesn't do any good to complain about the things we can't change.'

'That saves me from apologising for not sending you home earlier,' Brandt remarked, a glitter of amusement in his eyes.

'And that saves me from reminding you that you should have,' she returned in the same light vein, and immediately regretted her lapse into the kind of teasing rejoinders she and Ed had exchanged the previous weekend. She stepped rather quickly away from him. 'Excuse me while I call my room-mate so she won't start worrying about me.'

Joan felt his gaze following her as she hurried down the corridor to her office. Why can't he be fifty years old and married, she asked herself with a rueful sigh, or, at thirty-five, paunchy and balding instead of so compellingly magnetic?

Returning her coat to its hanger, she walked to her desk and dialled the telephone number of her apartment. On the second ring, Kay answered.

'Joan, where are you?' her room-mate demanded frantically.

'I'm at work,' she answered.

'I've been imagining you stuck somewhere in a snowbank like half the population of Chicago,' Kay sighed in relief. 'Isn't the boss going to bring you home?'

'In this blizzard?' Joan chided. 'We'd end up in a snowdrift!'

'Do you mean——' There was a pregnant pause before Kay continued. 'The two of you are stranded there at the office—alone?'

'Oh, Kay!' Joan pressed a weary hand to her forehead. 'Will you please not dramatise the situation?' She was having trouble enough with her own imagination without subjecting herself to Kay's.

'It is just the two of you there, isn't it?' Laughter bubbled in the voice on the other end. 'Thrown together by the elements!'

'Will you stop it?' Joan demanded with an exasperated sigh. 'Mr Lyon is my boss!'

'I bet you won't be calling him Mr Lyon by tomorrow morning!' Kay laughed aloud.

'For heaven's sake! For all the notice that Mr Lyon pays to me, I doubt if he's even aware that I'm a member of the opposite sex. I'm his efficient and practical secretary. Having my company forced on him for a day isn't going to make him suddenly discover that I'm an alluring female.' The outburst was more a reminder for herself than an attack on her room-mate. 'I have some letters to type now. I'll be home as soon as the roads are clear.'

Without waiting for a response, Joan hung up. Tension pulled down the corners of her mouth as she turned in her chair. Her downcast eyes caught sight of the brown trousers standing in front of her desk, and waves of crimson red swept into her face as she looked into Brandt Lyon's amused face and realised he had been listening. A muscle twitched near his mouth as if concealing a smile.

'It's comforting to discover you're human, Miss Somers,' he said quietly, and walked into his office while Joan was still searching for a response.

There wasn't any need to watch the clock, so she ignored the movements of her watch as she typed the dictation she hadn't been able to do earlier that day. She had no idea what Brandt was doing in his inner office, undoubtedly working the same as she. Her unfortunate conversation with Kay kept playing back in her mind. She grew more and more uncomfortable at the prospect of facing Brandt when her words were probably still ringing in his ears. They seemed such a cry for his attention that she wanted to run and hide.

With the headset covering her ears and Brandt's dictation occupying the rest of her thoughts, Joan didn't hear the connecting door open. The keys of the electric typewriter were racing across the paper. There wasn't a pause in the rhythm until a hand touched her shoulder. Her fingers crashed against the keys in surprise, jamming them against the ribbon.

'I didn't mean to frighten you, Miss Somers.' His head was tilted curiously to the side, his gaze studying the apprehensively withdrawn look in her brown eyes as she turned sharply towards him.

'Y-You startled me, that's all,' she stammered.

'I'm getting hungry and I thought you might direct me to the more edible items in the canteen. I hope you'll join me, Miss Somers.'

The light inflection he gave her name was a mocking reminder that he was aware of their status as employer and employee, and her sharp statement that she was his efficient and practical secretary.

Her own brown eyes bounced away from the strong lines of his face as she nervously glanced at her watch. Half past seven. If only she could hope that the rest of the time could pass so swiftly!

'Yes,' I'm hungry, too,' she answered, reverting to her cool professional voice in order to establish that impersonal business relationship she had once wanted to break down.

Brandt stepped back and waited for her to straighten her papers before joining him. She tried to make her muscles relax as she preceded him down the corridor to the canteen, but she knew she was holding her head unnaturally erect, driven by a need to show him that she didn't really want his attention. Her replies were just as stiff as he attempted to make light conversation over their less than glamorous meal of sandwiches, milk and potato chips.

Joan was rather thankful when he finally subsided into silence until she glanced up to discover he was watching her. A wary light crept into her brown eyes before she quickly looked away.

'It's your own fault, you know.' His baritone voice broke the silence.

It was really unnecessary to ask what he meant, but she did it anyway. 'What is?' she asked, widening her eyes with false innocence.

'The fact that I take you for granted,' Brandt

33

replied calmly, leaning back in his chair with an ease she couldn't begin to emulate. 'I mean, you hardly try to call attention to yourself.'

She played with a potato chip, the rosy glow in her cheeks adding a vibrancy to her face. 'I meant no disrespect this afternoon on the telephone. I truly don't expect any special recognition for doing my job. I mean, it's what I'm paid for.' She shifted uncomfortably in her chair.

'How old are you?'

'Twenty-three.' The last bite of sandwich seemed to be stuck to her throat.

'How long have you been working for me?'

'Three years.'

'That long?' A brow raised in surprise. 'You blend too well into the background.'

'A good secretary is supposed to,' Joan replied.

'It's never good to appreciate someone's efforts after they've left,' he responded smoothly. 'Which makes it difficult for me to take advantage of you now.'

'How?' The question was out before she could stop it and another fiery shade crimsoned her face.

The lines around his mouth deepened. 'I was going to ask if you would take some dictation tonight. There's little else but work to pass the hours. And this is a good time to catch up on some of the correspondence I've pushed to one side lately.'

'Of course I will. If I didn't have something to do, I would find it. I was on the last of the tapes when we came to eat.' Joan seized on the offer to put an end to their disturbing conversation and

34

quickly started gathering up the remains of their meal.

It was after ten o'clock when Brandt stopped suddenly in mid-sentence. Joan's pencil continued its rapid pace across the paper as she jotted down the last of his dictation.

'You must be exhausted,' Brandt commented, swinging his chair to look at her. 'Why didn't you stop me earlier?'

'It didn't seem necessary,' she answered, unconsciously flexing her tense fingers and loosening her death grip on the pencil.

'From the sound of the wind, we'll have all day tomorrow to finish whatever needs to be done. I think it's time we called it a night.'

The moment had arrived that Joan had been dreading all afternoon and evening. There was no need to mention that the building only possessed one couch, the one in Brandt Lyon's office. She knew instinctively that his basically gentlemanly nature would offer it to her, but she hadn't decided whether she should refuse and insist that he take it. Either way it turned out, Joan knew she wasn't going to be able to sleep a wink.

'Are you ready for the argument?' Brandt asked.

'What argument?' she breathed in sharply.

'Over which one of us is going to sleep on the only couch in the building,' he answered with a completely straight face. 'I know we could each sleep in a chair and solve the issue, but my mother would never forgive me if I didn't insist that you take the couch.'

'Really, I c——' Joan began, her hands raising to protest his statement.

'Yes, you could, and you will.' The quiet authority in his voice silenced the rest of her words. 'It's an order from the boss and a good secretary doesn't disobey an order.'

There was mockery in his words, but none in the voice that uttered them. Joan removed the tortoise-shell glasses that made it difficult to see his face clearly at that distance. She searched the implacable blue eyes for a tell-tale sign of amusement at the modesty that had sent her colour fluctuating wildly. His intent regard forced her to lower her gaze without finding the answer.

'If you insist, Mr Lyon.' The murmur of acceptance was drawn reluctantly from her lips.

'I do insist, Miss Somers.'

Strong fingers closed over the arms of his chair as Brandt pushed himself upright, flexing his shoulders as if he, too, felt the strain of a long day's work. Through her lashes, Joan studied the leanness of his build. His height, easily two inches over six feet, deceptively made the breadth of his chest seem not so intimidating as it really was.

In the summer months, Brandt Lyon spent few hours in the confines of his office and the long winter months didn't lessen the dark tan he had gained from long hours outdoors on various construction sites. The stamp of pride and quiet authority was in the chiselled, angular planes of his face, strikingly compelling like the piercing sharpness of an eagle.

As if sensing her surreptitious gaze, his head

swung around to her, one eyebrow rising a fraction of an inch. Her pulse fluttered erratically under his disturbing look. To cover her confusion, she began flipping the pages back on her shorthand pad to the first of his dictation.

'What are you doing, Miss Somers?'

She swallowed back the lump of nervousness to respond coolly. 'I'm going over these letters while they're still fresh in my mind.'

'Let them go until morning.' His hand waved the air in dismissal. 'If you have trouble deciphering them, you can ask me then. Besides,' one corner of his mouth was pulled upward, 'you know you can't read your notes without those glasses that are still on your lap.'

A furious rush of heat suffused her face as Joan quickly snapped the pad shut. The sudden movement sent her spare pencil flying across the room to land at his feet. Feeling like a gauche schoolgirl, she walked over to retrieve it from his outstretched hand, unable to meet the laughter she knew was in his eyes. As she bolted for the connecting door, the telephone rang.

'I'll answer it, Miss Somers,' he stated. His low voice was liberally laced with indulgent amusement.

The door between the two offices didn't latch securely after Joan had darted through it. The absence of any other sound in the building allowed his voice to carry clearly into the adjoining room.

After an initial impersonal greeting, the tone of his voice changed subtly to a more caressing sound as she heard him say: 'I should have thought it was obvious that I wouldn't keep our date tonight, Angela. Not that I wouldn't prefer being snowbound at your apartment for the weekend.'

The image of the petite blonde immediately danced into Joan's mind. The muscles of her stomach constricted painfully as she thought how aptly named the fragilely dainty girl was. There was a seductive pitch in the soft laughter that followed the pause after his statement. Swiftly Joan walked back and closed the door tightly between the two offices before she succumbed to the pangs of envy.

She busied her hands with emptying ashtrays and restraightening her already orderly desk until the light on her extension phone went out, signalling the end of the conversation. Within the span of a few seconds, the connecting door was opened and Brandt Lyon walked in.

'My office is yours, Miss Somers,' he said with a mocking sweep of his hand. 'You might want to use your coat as a pillow since the sofa doesn't have any.'

With a self-conscious nod of agreement, Joan walked around her desk to the coat tree, removed the three-quarter-length fun-fur coat and folded it in front of her like a shield. Even as she did it, she knew the gesture was silly, since Brandt Lyon had made it plain she had no cause to protect herself from him.

When she reached the open door, she glanced awkwardly over her shoulder. He held the troubled brown light in her eyes for an instant before walking behind her desk and settling his long form in the visitor's armchair.

'Goodnight, Miss Somers,' he said firmly, quenching any argument that might have been forming in her mind over their sleeping arrangements.

'Goodnight,' Joan answered in a voice that lacked conviction.

With the door closed behind her, she walked hesitantly to the long leather sofa. Drawing a deep breath, she arranged her coat in a plump square at one end and slipped off her shoes. The olive green jacket of her corduroy suit she laid over the back of a chair before removing the pins that held her long hair in place. The release of its weight was accompanied by a tired yawn.

Hoping that the yawn was a sign that sleep would not be denied her, Joan flicked off the switch of the overhead light, throwing the room into complete darkness. She felt her way back to the sofa and lay down.

The darkness and the emptiness of the building, save for the man in the outer office, closed around her. The howling wind sounded much louder than before as it vented its fury on the rattling window panes. The chair in her office creaked loudly and Joan could only guess that Brandt was settling into a more comfortable position.

It was more than an hour before her alertness receded and sleep crept slowly upon her. Even then it wasn't restful as a nightmarish dream claimed her subconscious.

In it, she was clinging to Ed Thomas, pleading with him not to send her back. A lion roared impatiently in the background. But Ed kept insisting that the lion was entitled to his share of her time and he pushed her in the direction of the unseen jungle beast.

When she tried to escape a large paw descended from the darkness and drew her back. The gargantuan proportions of the rumbling lion had Joan quaking with fear. As long as she stayed between the lion's paws, he ignored her, but whenever she attempted to sneak away, a mighty paw pulled her back. The lion's cobalt blue eyes saw her no matter where she hid.

Fear that she would never escape the lion enclosed her with icy fingers. Joan shuddered violently in its grip. 'Wake up. It's only a dream,' she kept telling herself, but that terrible coldness wouldn't go away. Finally her lashes fluttered open and she tried to penetrate the almost total darkness of the room to focus her eyes on some reassuring object that would end the reign of freezing terror.

The luminescent dial of her wristwatch gleamed at her, but still the numbness in her limbs didn't leave. She shivered again and hugged her arms tighter around her middle. As she drew a deep breath, the coldness of the air struck her. Tentatively she touched the sofa where the warmth of her body heat hadn't reached. The leather was icy cold.

Wrapping her coat around her shoulders, she rose to her feet and stumbled towards the door and the light switch beside it. Nothing happened when she flicked the switch on. The storm that was still raging outside had knocked out the electricity .

Quickly she opened the door between the two offices. 'Mr Lyon?' she whispered softly, trying to visualise in her mind the distance from the door to her desk. 'Mr Lyon?' she called again in a slightly louder voice.

A probing hand reached out into the darkness as she felt her way to the desk and then the chair. It was empty, with only a little warmth remaining in the cushions.

'Mr Lyon?' She nearly ran into the open door leading into the hallway. Her hand maintained contact with the corridor wall as she tiptoed into the dark void. 'Mr Lyon?'

Only the echo of her own voice and the whistling north wind answered her. She ventured further into the darkness, trying to fight off the sensation that she was completely alone in the building.

'Mr Lyon?' A frightened note crept into her cry. Where could he be? she wondered frantically, and called again, much louder this time. 'Mr Lyon? Brandt? Where are you? Brandt?'

A beam of light pinned her against a wall, blinding her as effectively as the darkness had done.

'There's no need to panic, Miss Somers. I'm right here,' Brandt Lyon's calm voice answered her.

Joan exhaled a shaky breath. 'I didn't panic. I ... I didn't know where you were,' she answered defensively. 'I called and called, but you didn't answer.'

'I'm sure you didn't panic,' he said dryly as he directed the blinding flashlight beam away from her face. 'I imagine it's common practice to run around in thirty-degree weather with bare feet.'

Instantly Joan was conscious of the cold tile floor

41

beneath her nylon-stockinged feet. An embarrassed warmth flooded her cheeks.

'I couldn't find my shoes in the dark,' she lied. 'Why didn't you answer when I called?' she asked as she wondered if he had heard the slip she had made when she had called him by his Christian name and decided that he had.

'I was in the basement verifying that the power failure wasn't caused by a blown fuse in the building.' His hand took hold of her elbow as he turned her back towards the offices. 'The storm must have knocked down a power line.'

Joan drew her coat tighter around her neck as she tried to ignore the warmth of his touch. 'Why isn't the furnace working? I mean, it's powered by natural gas.'

'Yes, but unfortunately the thermostat controls and the blower are electrically operated,' Brandt answered grimly. 'I'm afraid it's only going to get colder. Wait here a minute,' he ordered.

In the next instant the light was gone as a door closed. Joan was left shivering in the dark hall, her legs turning into numb sticks as the cold of the floor crept up her feet. Then the light gleamed on her again.

'What were you doing?' Her teeth had started to chatter.

'Turning on the taps in the rest-room so with luck the waterlines in the building won't freeze,' he answered. His hand again took hold of her elbow as they walked the last few feet to her office.

The carpeted floor felt blissfully warm compared to the coldness of the smooth tiles in the hallway.

The pressure of his hand didn't ease until they had entered Brandt's inner office. Joan walked unaided to the sofa, illuminated by the side reflection of his flashlight now shining on the sheepskin jacket in the back corner.

'What time is it?' she asked as she sat down on the cold leather cushions and curled her legs beneath her in an effort to warm her feet.

'Almost one-thirty.'

'Is that all?' She shivered and snuggled deeper into her coat. 'It will be below zero in here by morning with no heat. We'll freeze to death.'

A heavy silence followed her statement. Then Brandt walked slowly to the sofa, stopping in front of it to look gravely at her upturned face.

'We can keep warm,' he said quietly, 'together. It's the only logical thing to do.'

Her heart lodged somewhere in her throat as she stared at the unreadable expression in his eyes. She tried desperately to push her apprehensions aside at the thought of spending a night in his arms and make her reaction to his suggestion as normal and practical as his. But at this moment she wasn't looking at her employer; she was looking at a virilely attractive man.

When she finally commanded her voice to reply, it was shaky and weak. 'We can use both our coats as blankets.'

'I knew I could count on you to see the practical side of it,' Brandt smiled. That smile was nearly Joan's undoing.

Self-consciously she stretched out on the sofa, hugging the back cushion as much as she could while Brandt switched off the flashlight. Then he was spreading his coat over her legs. Joan rigidly held herself still as he lay down on the outer edge of the couch, turning on his side to face her. Her coat only partially covered him, but that thought was banished as the warmth of his body was pressed against her.

His arm slid around her waist to draw her closer, making her more fully aware of every muscular inch. The warmth of his breath was a soft caress against her cheek. Joan knew he could feel the rapid beating of her heart just as she felt the steady rhythm of his.

'Your feet are like ice cubes. You should have worn your shoes,' he murmured softly.

Instinctively Joan drew her toes away from the heavy material of his trouser legs, his intimate comment disturbing her more than the touch of his hands.

'Leave your feet there.' She felt the movement of his mouth as he spoke. 'They'll be warm soon.'

Since it was nearly impossible to find a place for her feet where they wouldn't touch him, Joan let them slide back to their former position as she wondered how she would ever relax enough to fall asleep.

CHAPTER THREE

DURING the night, their positions had shifted. Joan awoke to find her head resting on the shoulder opposite her, her face nearly buried in the fake fur collar of her coat. Her arms were curled around Brandt's middle in a careless embrace while his hands were locked behind her back to hold her there. Gradually she became conscious of his face buried in the length of her amber hair.

She tried to move into a less intimate position, only to have the pressure of his arms increase. Her corduroy skirt had inched up around her thighs, making her doubly aware of the muscles in his legs. Brandt stirred beneath her and she held her breath.

'Whoever it was,' he said softly, his voice husky with sleep, 'that first complained about getting out of a warm bed on a cold morning certainly knew what he was talking about.'

'Yes,' Joan agreed breathlessly, 'b-but w-we can't stay here all day.'

'Why not?' The corners of his mouth were turned upward against her hair. Then the chest beneath her head raised as he took a deep breath and loosened his hold around her. 'You're right. We can't stay here all day.'

Joan twisted backwards, balancing herself on one arm to allow him room to get up. Frigid air penetrated the warmth that had been generated between them. As Brandt slid from beneath the cover of their coats on to the floor, Joan resisted the impulse to snuggle into the warmth of her coat.

'Don't get up.' His hand pushed her back on the sofa when she started to rise. 'Stay there and keep warm as long as you can.'

'What are you going to do?' she frowned.

The freezing temperature of the room was biting her face and nose, but Brandt seemed impervious to it as he stood above her in his rumpled suit, an aura of charged vitality about him that wasn't easy to dismiss.

'If I remember correctly there's a catalytic heater at the shack in the equipment yard,' he replied in his take-charge voice.

Joan glanced towards the window, white frost covering the panes, but the wind growled fiercely on the other side. If it had stopped snowing in the night, the wind would still be blowing the fallen snow reducing visibility to near zero.

'Do you have to go out?' she asked anxiously.

His mouth moved into a lazy smile, making it difficult to breathe properly. 'I'll follow the fence to the shack. I won't get lost.'

No, Joan thought shakily, he wouldn't get lost. Even in a battle with the elements, Brandt Lyon would probably come out the victor. But she had been brought up in the north. She knew how dangerous it could be to venture out in a storm of this magnitude. People had been known to become lost within a few feet of safety. The velvet depths of her eyes shimmered with her fear.

Instantly the smile vanished from Brandt's face and there was a hard, purposeful set to his strong jaw. 'Don't get carried away by your imagination,' he said a shade curtly. 'I'll need my coat, so you'll have to curl up in your own until I get back.'

As he reached for his sheepskin jacket, Joan tried to draw her legs beneath her coat, but it was too short. Before she could shift into a half-sitting position with her legs curled beneath her, Brandt had removed his coat, revealing the bareness of her legs where her skirt had ridden up. She flushed uncomfortably as she quickly hid them under her coat.

'Don't be embarrassed,' Brandt drawled in mockery. 'You have very nice legs.'

'Y-You'd better ... t-take my scarf,' Joan stammered, sneaking a hand from under her coat to brush the hair from her cheek, wishing he didn't have the ability to disconcert her so easily.

The grey wool scarf was sticking out of the pocket of her coat. Brandt removed it, then reached over and crooked a finger under her chin to raise it.

'Stop worrying,' he commanded firmly. 'I'll be back before you have a chance to miss me.'

Joan doubted that. The instant the office door closed, a frightening sense of desertion spread over her. It was this aloneness that made her huddle deeper into her coat and not the biting nip of the air stinging her nose. The minutes passed with interminable slowness as she listened intently for some slight sound signifying his return. The impulse was there to wait for him by the rear door, but her practical nature wouldn't let her give in to it. Without the benefit of his body heat, she was already beginning to feel the cold stealing in. With no cover for her legs, she would rapidly succumb to the chilling temperature if she strayed from the sofa.

Twenty minutes went by before she heard his footsteps in the outer corridor. Her lashes fluttered down in relief, only to fly open when the human snowman walked into the office. Snow caked the trouser legs and only patches of brown could be seen on the sheepskin of his jacket. The brown thickness of his hair was capped with white flakes, the same flakes that clung to his brows and lashes. His hoary breath filled the room with billowing clouds.

The determined set of his rugged features had been moulded by the storm. They didn't vary, but his blue eyes smiled at her brightly in triumph as he sat the small heater on the floor.

'You found it,' Joan murmured, finding she couldn't voice her relief at his safe return.

His broad shoulders blocked her view of the heater as he knelt beside it. Within a few minutes, Joan felt the first emanations of heat. The snow on his clothes began to melt, puddles forming on the carpet.

'You're going to catch pneumonia in those wet things,' she said anxiously.

'That's an old wives' tale,' Brandt declared, shrugging out of his jacket like a giant grizzly bear coming out of hibernation. 'Pneumonia is caused by a germ, not wet clothes. It'll be uncomfortable for a while, but they'll soon dry.' He walked to the sofa, picked up her shoes sitting on the floor beside it, and carried them back to the heater. 'We'll get them warm before you have to put them on,' he explained.

His thoughtfulness sent a warm glow of pleasure through her veins. That combination of indomitable strength and tender consideration was rare. Perhaps, Joan decided, when someone was as self-assured as Brandt Lyon, they could afford to show such kindness without fearing damage to their male ego.

Her eyes followed his movements as he used her scarf to rub most of the snow from his hair and carelessly brushed the flakes that hadn't melted from his slacks. Before she could conceal her silent study of him, his gaze glittered over her.

'This heater isn't going to be able to keep both rooms warm. We'll have to decide which office we're going to use,' he stated.

'I won't be able to type those letters you dictated since there isn't any electricity, but I had thought I would take out the inactive folders from the filing cabinet,' Joan offered hesitantly. The prospect of sitting idle the entire day with Brandt Lyon's dominating presence was too daunting to contemplate.

'It's settled. We'll move the heater into your office.' He reached down for her shoes and handed them to her. 'I'll go open a window.'

'A window?' she blinked in confusion.

His gaze trailed over while she slipped on her warmed shoes. 'The heater burns the oxygen in the air. We'll need some ventilation if we don't want to suffocate.'

An hour later the temperature in Joan's office had increased to the point where she no longer needed to wear her heavy coat to be comfortable. Brandt had disappeared again on an undisclosed errand after setting up the portable typing table in her office. Pausing for a moment beside the heater to warm her fingers, Joan wondered how she would have fared if she had been stranded alone, dependent on her own resourcefulness.

The door to the hall opened and closed quickly, a cold draught accompanying Brandt. She glanced curiously at the tray in his hands.

'Without electricity, we can't have coffee, but when this thaws, we'll have sweet rolls and juice, courtesy of the canteen,' he announced.

'I wish you hadn't mentioned coffee,' Joan grimaced, walking around her desk to rummage through the centre drawer for her comb. 'I never feel myself in the mornings until I've had my first cup.'

'Yourself being the cool efficient paragon who rules the office?' Brandt questioned, a brow arching with complacent amusement.

The comb in her hand faltered in mid-stroke through the slightly tangled locks of her long hair.

'I don't rule the office,' Joan asserted, feeling more like a schoolgirl than an efficient secretary as her cheekbones gleamed with a rosy hue of embarrassment.

'You blush very easily, don't you?'

The colour intensified. 'It has something to do with being fair-skinned, I think.' She kept her head averted from his discerning eyes as she began winding her hair into its prim coil at the nape of her neck.

'Leave your hair down,' he commanded huskily, covering the distance between them when she wasn't looking. 'It'll keep your ears warm. Besides——' His fingers pulled part of her hair free from her unresisting hold, and Joan was too startled by his sudden nearness to protest. 'The colour of your hair is much too attractive to be concealed in that severe style. It's like spun gold when it's loose.'

'It's naturally that colour,' she stated as if he had accused her of achieving the colour from a bottle.

He laughed softly. 'I guessed that.'

Joan fought back the clamouring of her senses. 'It's too unpractical to wear it down. It keeps getting in the way.'

'Does it?' Disbelief was in his question as he tucked her hair behind her ears and turned away. 'You never wear it down so how can you be sure?'

'You'll see,' she declared, shaking the rest of her hair free in frustration and dumping the pins on top of the desk.

The instant she surrendered to his stronger will, she knew she had made an irretrievable mistake. The cloud of hair about her shoulders made her feel instinctively feminine and vulnerable, the very sensations she needed to avoid or she would fall completely under the power of his magnetism. The invisible barrier between employer and employee had been breached last night when she had lain in his arms. She desperately needed to repair her defences.

With cold deliberateness, she ignored him the rest of the morning, completing the filing from the wire basket on her desk. On the surface, Joan was successful, but an inner radar kept her apprised of every movement Brandt made as he pored over the blueprint spread out on the draughting table.

'I'm hungry.' His low voice shattered the silence, causing Joan to spin abruptly around. 'What are we having for lunch?'

The blue depths of his eyes seemed to pull her into a whirlpool of emotional chaos. This strange intimacy that had crept between them made it nearly impossible for her to react naturally. Bells rang, warning her that she was becoming much too susceptible to his attraction, but she couldn't think of what she might do to prevent it.

'I don't know,' she answered quickly, turning back to the file drawers before she succumbed to despair at her own vulnerability.

'I'll see what the canteen has to offer.'

As she nibbled the cold sandwich later, Joan realised it was this constant sharing that was destroying her peace of mind. A business aloofness couldn't be maintained in these circumstances. She was conscious of his stirring interest in her or maybe it was curiosity as Brandt regarded her in a new light. discovering the humanness behind her façade of efficiency.

But wasn't she making too much of his new interest? What harm would there be in a friendship being developed between them? What was there to fear? If Brandt Lyon did begin to regard her as a woman, that didn't mean he was suddenly going to be overwhelmed by her average looks — not when someone like Angela lurked in his memory.

'A penny for your thoughts,' Brandt's voice snapped the thread of her musings.

'They aren't worth it,' Joan protested self-consciously.

'Anything that can keep a woman quiet for fifteen minutes must be worth at least a penny,' he mocked.

'If you must know.' She glanced up from her sandwich into the vivid blue of his eyes, now lazily veiled by thick lashes. 'I was wondering how much longer the storm would last.'

'Getting tired of my company already?'

'Not as tired as you must be of mine,' Joan retorted, not able to match the lightness in his voice.

'On the contrary.'-There was an eloquent shrug of his broad shoulders. 'As a matter of fact, I was just wondering how an attractive girl like you has avoided the altar.'

'It's more a case of the altar avoiding me.'

'Then you aren't a career girl.' The smoothly firm line of his mouth was pulled into a wry smile. 'That means some day I'll have to find myself another secretary, and just when I was becoming used to you, too.'

'I haven't handed in my notice yet, Mr Lyon,' Joan said stiffly.

'It was Brandt last night,' he reminded her with a wicked light in his eyes. Their dancing gleam was disturbing and Joan looked away. 'Surely there's someone special in your life, isn't there? Or would you have me believe that you dress sexily for a maiden aunt?'

She blinked back the sudden sting of tears, pride surfacing with a rush. She couldn't tell him of her empty weekends, of the countless nights she had spent in her own company. Those half-forgotten words she had spoken last week when she had intimated that her weekends were always occupied had come back to haunt her. White lies or any kind of lies always seemed to compound into more.

'I don't know if——' Joan hesitated, then plunged forward, hoping she wasn't burying herself in a series of lies and silently apologising to Ed Thomas for seeking refuge in his name, '——Ed is exactly special, but I am fond of him.' That statement was at least the truth.

'Have you known him long?' The tilt of the leonine head indicated a casual interest.

'No, he's a brother of my room-mate's fiancé.' Her fingers were tearing nervously at the uneaten portion of her sandwich.

'Your room-mate is the Moreland girl in the computer department, isn't she?'

'Yes, that's right, Kay Moreland,' Joan answered in a startled voice that betrayed her surprise. She had never suspected that he was even aware she had a room-mate.

'Are you bringing Ed to the Christmas party?'

'Well, actually,' his question had caught her off guard, 'he lives in Cleveland.'

'It must be pretty serious if he flies back and forth just to see you,' Brandt commented.

'And his brother,' Joan added, rising to her feet in an effort to end the conversation.

The swivel chair behind her desk squeaked loudly in protest to her sudden movement, screeching like chalk on a blackboard.

'That chair needs to be oiled,' he said, walking over to rock it back and forth.

'I may look like an Amazon, but that chair is too heavy for me to turn upside down to get to the area where the squeak is,' she said sharply.

There was a piercing quality to the look he gave her, the harshness of controlled anger. Her chin tilted defiantly as she swallowed the tight lump in her throat. Joan had always been conscious of her size ever since her teenage days when she had towered over the boys in her class.

His eyes narrowed as he studied her. 'Have you always been sensitive about your height?'

'It isn't something that can be ignored,' Joan responded stiffly.

'Why is it,' Brandt's head was cocked inquiringly to the side, 'that short girls always dream of being statuesque and tall girls want to be daintily petite?'

'It's human nature, I suppose,' she shrugged, 'to want what you can't have. But I have accepted the way I am.'

'Then stop apologising for being a tall, beautiful blonde.' The crisply spoken compliment seemed to accuse her of false modesty and Joan reacted sharply.

'Really, Mr Lyon, you can't expect me to believe you!' Her head was thrown back in an indignant pose. 'In the three years I've worked for you, you've never once paid any attention to me as more than your secretary.'

Brandt's knee was hooked over the corner of her desk as he half sat and half stood against it, his hands folded complacently on his thigh.

'You have only yourself to blame for that. The "No Trespassing" signs were so boldly displayed and your manner was so briskly efficient and businesslike that I couldn't guess that you wanted to be treated as a woman. Besides,' a latent harshness crept into his strong features, 'I've always lived by the rule that business should never become mixed with pleasure. I don't want my personal life to be intertwined with my work.'

The precise. clearly spoken statement sent prickles up her spine. Joan no longer doubted that he was sincere. Brandt Lyon did consider her attractive. At the same time, he made it clear that her looks made no difference. He would never want her as more than his secretary. And she had to accede to the advisability of his stand. If a man—woman relationship had developed between them and later burned itself out. her position in his office would have become untenable for both of them.

She averted her gaze from the determined line of his jaw. 'I agree with you completely.' Her mouth moved stiffly in resistance to the words she uttered.

A heavy sigh of exasperation sounded behind her

and she faintly caught a whispering 'Do you?' that was mockingly derisive. Pushing aside her long hair, Joan glanced over her shoulder, a bewildered frown knitting creases in her forehead. His back was turned to her as he tilted the chair back, then completely turned it upside down.

'Do you have any all-purpose oil here?' he asked.

The detached voice forced Joan to conclude she had only imagined the previous question, a trick of her imagination that was so susceptible to Brandt's masculinity.

'In the middle desk drawer,' she answered.

While Brandt worked at oiling the squeaky springs of the swivel chair, Joan began sorting through the file cabinet, removing the inactive folders and placing them on a nearby straight chair. Only one part of her mind was devoted to the task. The rest was trying to draw comfort from the discovery that Brandt thought she was attractive.

Her preoccupation made her less thorough in her actions. She barely noticed that the top drawer didn't close tightly when she pushed it forward to go through the second drawer. Her mouth twitched in amusement as she found a folder misfiled. It was one she had given Brandt the other day and he had replaced it in the wrong drawer. Removing it from its incorrect place, she reached down for the third drawer of the four-drawer cabinet.

The instant her fingers released the catch on the drawer handle and began to pull it open, the un-latched top drawer began sliding forward. A pro-testing groan sounded as the combined weight of the three drawers was exerted on the metal cabinet. That was the only warning Joan received before it tilted forward. Her hands reached out uselessly to try to check its fall, succeeding for a second to keep it at an angle.

Then strong arms were lending their power to hers, righting the cabinet and pushing the drawers back into place. The after-shock of realizing how very near she had come to having the cabinet fall on top of her sent shudders of fright through her now trembling limbs. Her knees felt incredibly weak and incapable of supporting her. Then those same strong hands that had saved her were gripping her shoulders.

'Are you all right, Joan?' There was a frown of sincere concern in the face bending towards her.

A trembling hand brushed her brow. 'Yes,' she answered shakily, 'I think so.' His shirt button blurred in front of her eyes as she unconsciously swayed closer to him. 'It ... It all happened so quickly.'

'Why did you try to stop it?' There was a hint of anger in Brandt's husky voice. 'You should have let it fall and worried about cleaning up the mess afterwards rather than risk injuring yourself!'

'I didn't think,' Joan answered with a choked sob.

His soft chuckle resembled a rueful sigh as he folded her comfortingly against his chest. 'You silly little fool,' he declared with a laugh. 'You're much too trusting. I always knew that monster would turn on you one of these days.'

Joan smiled weakly into his shirt, her fingers curling around the lapels of his suit jacket. His lighthearted reference to the filing cabinet eased the inner quaking. But as the shivers of near-catastrophe subsided, they were replaced by a tingling awareness of his embrace.

Being within the strong circle of his arms was no accident of sleep. Motionless, she savoured the beat of his heart beneath her hand and the firm pressure of his thighs against her body. A languorous warmth began spreading from the hands on her back. She felt his face move through the golden silkiness of her hair to halt near her ear.

Her stilted breathing told her she should break free from his embrace, however innocent it was. But the exhilarated sensation of bliss was unknown to her, a frightening kind of excitement that lured her to remain. This taste of wild honey was bitter-sweet as if she were drinking a nectar that was exclusively for the gods.

'Are you certain you weren't hurt?'

His calm voice almost made Joan wish she could lay claim to an injury, but she sensibly shook her head that she wasn't. Her hands stiffened against his chest as she pushed herself away, or at least as far away as the hands on her back would permit.

'I'm all right, really.' Her mouth moved into a nervous smile of assurance.

Without her glasses, the closeness of his roughly stamped features was a blur. Yet her awareness of the nearness of his mouth sent her pulse racing as she wondered what it would be like if Brandt kissed her. There was something about him that made her think he would be very good at making love, quite beyond her experience. Her lashes

59

fluttered down so that her expressive brown eyes wouldn't reveal the direction her thoughts had taken.

His hand left her shoulder blades to brush back the long hair that had fallen over her cheek. 'I like the perfume you're wearing,' Brandt mused absently. 'It suits you.'

'I ... I'm not wearing any perfume,' Joan answered in an embarrassed whisper, again at a loss as to how to cope with his indifferently intimate remarks.

'You're not?' His tanned face moved downward to the side of her neck where she was acutely conscious of his soft inhalation along her skin. 'It must be the clean fragrance of your hair.' He shrugged and released her.

'I—I suppose it is,' she agreed, turning away to conceal the confused pain that glittered in her eyes. She pushed back the length of her hair so it cascaded down her back. 'I shampooed it only the other night.'

If Ed or any other man she knew had made such a comment, Joan would have laughed it off, but with Brandt, she paradoxically resented it. She wished she had been wearing some provocative perfume. The term 'clean fragrance' always reminded her of a baby that had been freshly bathed, and she didn't like the idea of Brandt regarding her as an infant.

'From now on,' Brandt's lithe strides had carried him back to her desk and the overturned chair, 'you'd better open only one drawer of that metal monster at a time.'

A rush of angry heat filled her cheeks. 'I hardly did it on purpose before!'

He turned slowly around, studying her with disconcerting thoroughness. 'I never said that you did, Joan.'

The calm usage of her Christian name, not spoken in a flash of concern, added to the upheaval of her senses. His slightly reproving tone filled her with a sick nervousness.

'I—I only m-meant——' she stammered her embarrassment.

'I know very well what you meant,' Brandt responded with a vague air of amusement. 'I know when a woman is tricking me into holding her in my arms.'

There was little she could say in return without sticking her foot in her mouth again. As Joan turned around to resume her work, she felt as small as a toothpick and not nearly as useful.

CHAPTER FOUR

In a forgotten corner of a cupboard, Brandt had found a box of candles. The flames of four were bravely fending off the encroaching darkness in Joan's office. Their wavering light was not sufficient to work by, but it had illuminated their—what had become tasteless fare—meal of sandwiches and chips.

Brandt was behind her desk, leaning back in the now silently unprotesting swivel chair, while Joan inexpertly puffed on the cigarette he had lit for her. Her nerves were still raw from their early afternoon encounter and she accepted the cigarette to give her trembling hands something to do, doubting that the nicotine would in any way calm her.

'Tell me about your family, Joan. Do they live in Chicago?' His gaze roamed over her face, not missing the way she avoided meeting his eyes.

He was making small talk, filling in the gaping silence of her unease. Conversation was necessary, if for no other reason than to keep her wayward thoughts in check. Answering his questions might take her mind off the softening effect the candlelight was having on his carved face. It seemed to heighten his attraction and make her more aware of his sensual virility.

'No, my parents live in a little town about ninety miles from here,' she answered in response to his question. 'I have an older brother in the service. He's stationed in Germany right now. My younger brother is in his last year of high school and my baby sister is in her first year, so they're both living at home.'

'What does your father do?'

'He and my mother run a small general store. It's a family affair. Jean and Bob, my sister and brother, help out after school and on weekends.' The smile she gave him was hesitant.

'It sounds like a very warm, settled environment.' Brandt leaned forward to crush out his cigarette, his gaze flicking smoothly over her face. 'You aren't the type to crave the excitement of the big city. What brought you to Chicago?'

'The secretarial college. When I graduated, there weren't any job openings in my home town, so I stayed on here.'

'It can be lonely without family and friends,' he commented.

Joan knew just how lonely it could be. 'I've made quite a few friends and I visit my family once a month,' she said defensively.

Brandt leaned back in his chair, smiling absently. 'I guess I've become accustomed to having my parents nearby. You've met my mother, haven't you?'

'Yes,' she admitted, remembering the day the tall, angular woman had entered her office, a feminine version of her son, not attractive, but compelling. She had been very warm and friendly to Joan, not treating her with a superior attitude.

'My father is a doctor,' Brandt continued in that same thoughtfully absent air. 'Semi-retired, working mostly as a consultant now, but he'll never quit completely. He enjoys his work too much.'

'I thought Lyon Construction was a company that had been started by your father.'

'My uncle. He passed away a few years ago. I worked for him in the summers when I was a kid, went to college, studied engineering and construction, and joined the firm when I graduated.'

'Do you have any brothers or sisters?' Her curiosity about his personal life was now undeniably aroused.

'A sister. Venetia followed in Dad's footsteps and became a doctor. She's practising in Arizona.'

'Hasn't she married?'

'No, she's a solitary like myself.' There was a dark glow emanating from the depths of his eyes as he arched a glance at her. 'Aren't you going to comment on the loneliness of a bachelor's life?'

'I can hardly throw stones when I live in a glass house,' Joan murmured.

'Don't you want to marry, settle down, and raise a family?' Brandt probed.

'I suppose.' She shifted uncomfortably in her chair. 'But that decision has to wait for the right man.'

'Haven't you met him yet? What about this Ed you mentioned before?' The movement sideways of her head indicated her reluctance to answer his questions and Brandt's mouth moved into a smile of rueful apology. 'I've become too personal, haven't I? I wouldn't want to answer a leading question like that myself. You——' he paused as his gaze narrowed in a swift appraisal of her downcast face, '——you don't quite have the look of a woman in love, that soft radiance that usually accompanies the other symptoms.'

'You make it sound like a disease.' She tried to laugh off his astute observation.

'In some ways it is. The loss of appetite, the restlessness, the funny aches, the pains of uncertainty.'

'You sound as if you know.' The fragile image of the blonde named Angela immediately leaped into Joan's mind and she experienced one of those funny aches that Brandt had just mentioned.

'A nodding acquaintance,' he smiled dryly, and rolled lightly to his feet, walking over to the outside window and staring through the frosted panes. 'It sounds as if the wind is letting up. Maybe the storm will blow itself out tonight.'

Jean gazed at the broad shoulders tapering to slim hips. What would it be like when the storm was over? she wondered. Would she return to being Miss Somers? Or had they progressed to a point where it would be impossible to return to that level of business aloofness?

She was afraid they had. In fact, she was afraid her own emotions had gone beyond the point where she could control them. Her reserve had been penetrated. That fragile defence barrier that had kept a safe distance between her and Brandt was gone.

'At least, we'll be warm tonight,' she said with false brightness, glancing at the heater sitting in the middle of the room.

'Not from the heater, we won't.' Brandt's denial was made so quietly that she wasn't certain she had understood what he said.

'What?' Her faltering voice asked the broad shoulders for clarification.

He twisted sideways, the flickering candle flames only partially exposing his face. An eyebrow was thoughtfully raised as his eyes, looking darker than their normal blue shade, inspected her wary expression.

'We won't be able to leave the heater on all night, Joan.'

'Why not?' Her eyes widened in bewildered protest. 'I mean, we can leave the window open for ventilation.'

'There isn't any risk of suffocation.' Brandt turned the rest of the way and walked back into the light, stopping beside her chair to study her upturned face. 'We haven't enough fuel to last through the night and into tomorrow and we can't be sure when the electricity will be restored.'

Joan stared at her hands, forcing them not to twist into the tight knots her stomach was in. Sensibly, logically, she wanted to admit that Brandt was being practical, but she didn't even have to close her eyes to visualise the sensation of lying by his side.

'I didn't know.' She nervously moistened her parched lips.

'I didn't tell you.' The bland expression on his

66

face made his inner thoughts unreadable. 'There wasn't any need to worry you unnecessarily.'

'I wouldn't have worried exactly,' murmured Joan, her quick glance skittering off his face.

Brandt continued staring at her, his gaze riveted on the shimmer of her moist lips in the candlelight. His hands were thrust in the pockets of his trousers, pushing open the suit jacket and emphasising the muscular flatness of his stomach. Then he inhaled deeply and pivoted away.

'I'll get our coats and warm them in front of the heater before we call it a night,' he announced as he briskly opened the inner office door.

The sudden draught of cold air sent little shudders quaking over Joan's skin. There was no objection she could raise, not when she had willingly agreed to the same arrangement the night before. The night before! It seemed as if a week had passed since yesterday. A little more than twenty-four hours ago she had been in complete charge of her unadventurous life. Now she felt insecure and lost, trapped in a course that had her slowly twisting in the wind.

Her heart was pounding against her ribs like a jackhammer when Brandt re-entered the room with their coats in his arms. She wished desperately that she could steal a bit of his calmness, but then he wasn't affected by her the way she was by him. No man had ever made her senses come alive the way Brandt did.

Joan felt the need to speak, but the impulse died in her throat as Brandt glanced at her and smiled, a lazy smile that seemed to understand her schoolgirl apprehensions. She chided herself for worrying. It was all one-sided.

Rising to her feet, she helped him drape the coats over the side chairs so the inner linings would be exposed to the heat. When that was completed, she clasped her hands together, holding them above the heater as if they were cold.

'I almost wish we'd decided to use your office today so at least the room would be warm.' Her mouth curved weakly into a smile.

'If the sofa wasn't so heavy and cumbersome, I'd move it in here.' Brandt's gaze was centred on the middle point between her shoulderblades. She could sense it as surely as if she had eyes in the back of her head. 'In a few minutes,' he continued in that same quiet, assuring voice, 'I'll take the heater in my office and get the worst of the chill off the room.'

If there had been a clock in the room, Joan didn't think its ticking could have drowned out the sound of her heartbeat. Last night there hadn't been any real opportunity to dwell on the thought of sleeping with Brandt. There had been no premeditation involved. Now, knowing that within a few minutes she would be walking into the office, slipping off her shoes and lying down on the sofa to wait for Brandt to stretch his form beside her, she feared she would betray her intense awareness of him.

She started visibly when Brandt stepped forward to remove the coats from the chairs. Except for a darting glance, he made no comment as he wrapped the jackets together to retain their heat. Behind the veil of her lashes, she watched him pick up the heater and carry it into his office.

When he hadn't returned in a few minutes, Joan knew she couldn't wait any longer. Her nerves were already scraped and raw. Extinguishing all but one candle, she draped the coats over her arm and picked up the remaining lit candle.

'Leave the door open,' Brandt said, not even glancing up when she entered the room.

He was bending over the heater and she could only guess that he was turning it off. She sat the candle on the table beside the sofa, not letting her gaze be pulled by the magnetic attraction of his presence. The air in the room was still decidedly brisk, but much warmer than it had been.

'I'll go and shut the window in your office while you get ready.' His voice came from the direction of the open door.

'Okay,' acknowledged Joan, since there seemed to be a necessity for a reply to his clipped statement.

Taking up her position along the back of the sofa, she arranged the coat over her legs and was trying to keep an ample amount of the top coat available for Brandt when he softly entered the office. There was an electric quality about the air, like the charged moments before a thunderstorm.

The candle was blown out, draping the room in darkness. For a moment Joan was completely blinded by the lack of light. Then there was the supple controlled movement as Brandt's weight was lowered on to the cushions. Instinctively she held her breath, bracing herself for the contact

69

with his hard form. There was no hesitation in the way he familiarly settled himself beside her, adjusting the curves of her body to fit his. Her breathing, when it returned, came in fitful spasms of blissful pain at being so near and forcing herself not to reveal the effect he had on her.

'Comfortable?' he asked with a deep husky quality to his voice that caressingly moved the air near her face.

'Yes,' Joan breathed with difficulty.

'It's warmer than last night.' The light tone was supposed to relax her.

'Yes,' she answered again, but it was the heat in her cheeks and neck that was causing her the most discomfort. A fire seemed to have been kindled somewhere in her mid-section.

'Goodnight, Joan,' Brandt said at last.

'Goodnight ... Brandt.' She couldn't help hesitating over his name. Yet, in the circumstances, it seemed ludicrous to refer to him as Mr Lyon.

Closing her eyes, she listened to and felt the steady rise and fall of his chest. Her nose was intoxicated by the strange mingling of tobacco smoke, spicy after-shave lotion and his heady masculine scent. She prayed for sleep to deaden her senses. Her muscles ached from trying to hold herself away from him, or at least not to relax against him.

His right arm was resting lightly over her waist. Unbidden the thought came to her, wondering what it would be like to be the recipient of his caresses. A quicksilver shudder of delight danced over her skin to her shoulders.

'Are you cold?' Brandt inquired softly.

Automatically her head moved in the direction of his voice, freezing abruptly when her cheek encountered his mouth and chin. 'A little,' she lied, unable to explain it any other way.

He edged the rest of his body closer, scorching her skin through the material of her clothes. There didn't seem any part of him that wasn't touching her and filling her with dangerous longings. Her heart stopped, then started again with a swift rush.

'Is that better?' The movement of his mouth against her cheek, so very close to the corner of her mouth, seemed to paralyse her.

The affirmative 'yes' was choked from her parched throat.

'What's the matter?' The soft guarded tone added to her confusion.

Opening her darkening eyes, Joan tried uselessly to focus them on the face next to her. 'Nothing,' she denied, but in a weak, faltering voice.

In an effort to free herself from the disturbing closeness of his mouth, she drew her head back into the corner of the sofa, keeping her face towards him. His right hand left her waist to brush the tangle of amber from her cheek.

'You're trembling,' he accused gently.

'Please, it's nothing,' she whispered. Tears of humiliation burned her eyes.

'I don't accept that, Joan,' he said flatly.

'Please, let's just go to sleep, Brandt,' she insisted with a throbbing quiver in her voice.

'Not until you tell me what's wrong.'

The firmness of his low voice sent a bubble of

71

hysteria into her throat to lodge there. How could she possibly tell him she wanted him to make love to her, to feel the caress of his hands and the warmth of his lips?

'Brandt.' The aching sigh of his name was more revealing than she realised.

The sudden tenseness of his muscles was communicated immediately to her. In the darkness she could only sense the slow movement of the head beside her as it came closer. Her lips trembled at the light touch of his mouth against them, feather light, not a kiss but a hesitant caress.

When his mouth moved an inch away, it was the moment to rebuff his advance. But she couldn't. She had fought so long against his attraction that she simply didn't have the willpower to deny it any longer.

His hand curved around the side of her neck, his fingers curling into her hair as he raised her head the fraction of an inch that was needed to meet his descending mouth. There was a bursting wave of heat at the immediate possession of his kiss, a dazzling unleashing of explosions.

As his body weight shifted above her, Joan slipped her arms around his waist, spreading her fingers over the taut muscles of his back. His mastery and sensuous passion gave him unlimited power and she moaned softly in surrender as the command of his mouth parted her lips. She was a captive, a willing slave to his wishes, and Brandt rewarded her by letting her see the dizzying heights.

But it wasn't only with her lips that he demanded a response. The gentle exploratory caress of his hands was deliberately kindling more flames in the rest of her body, slowly building to a crescendo that would match the urgency of his hunger. Yet his very gentleness, his sureness persuaded her to sweep aside any fear.

When his fingers undid the last button of her blouse and pushed the material aside, Joan could only sigh with gratification at the touch of his hand on the rounded curve of her breast. The heady gloriousness, the supreme sense of rightness at what was happening, banished all modesty. The whole universe could have collapsed at that moment and she would not have cared as long as she was in Brandt's strong arms.

As his mouth ravaged the hollow of her throat, beginning a slow meandering trail to the shadowy cleft between her breasts, a bursting light filled the room. For a moment, Joan thought she had only imagined the sudden illumination of light on her closed eyes. Then the cessation of Brandt's caress prompted her to open her eyes. The fluorescent overhead lights were on!

His head remained buried in her neck for an instant longer. Then he cursed briefly beneath his breath and pushed himself upright and away from her. She stared at him in tortured stillness, watching him as he sat on the edge of the sofa, his breathing ragged and uneven, raking his hands through his brown hair before using them to cover his face.

'That's as effective as the cold light of day!'

The bitterly spoken words drew a silent gasp of

dismay from Joan. Brandt felt nothing but regret. The desire had been of the moment only, and intense shame washed over her. Foolishly she had thought his passion had been sparked by more than just lust.

Hot tears of humiliation scalded her cheeks as she fumbled beneath her coat with the buttons of her blouse, her skin still betrayingly tingling from the intimate caresses of his hands on her nakedness.

'Joan, I'm sorry.' His low voice rumbled from some deep, dark pit. 'You must think I'm——'

'Please don't apologise!' She lashed out sharply, knowing she couldn't bear to be degraded any further. 'It really isn't necessary!'

Partially covered, sufficient for modesty's sake, she pushed herself upright on the sofa, driven by an overwhelming need to run before the heat in her cheeks was drowned by a gulf of tears. Before she could complete the movement that would bring her to her feet, Brandt's arm was pinioning her against the sofa, his fingers digging roughly into the flesh of her arm.

'You aren't going anywhere.' Blue fires blazed in his eyes, their flames licking over her startled face and the lips warm and swollen by his kisses. 'Not until we talk this over.'

The hard set of his features indicated the tight hold he had on his temper and emotions. The sight of his masculinely carved face could still raise havoc with her senses, but she kept her expression cold and proud.

'There isn't anything to talk about,' she stated, refusing to flinch under his painful grip.

'You damn well know there is!' It was spoken softly, almost under his breath.

'Please.' But the polite word was not spoken as a plea as she reached up to push his hand away from her arm. 'You're putting too much importance on what happened.'

'What nearly happened, you mean,' Brandt reminded her with a cutting edge to his tongue.

In spite of herself, colour stained her cheeks in admission and she quickly averted her head, letting her tousled hair fall forward to cover her face.

'But it didn't happen,' she added firmly. 'We're both normal, healthy human beings who happen to be members of the opposite sex,' she argued logically, trying to regain some measure of her own self-respect. 'Propinquity and an unusual situation simply prompted us to do things we wouldn't have done in normal circumstances.'

'Do you believe that?' His eyes narrowed as he withdrew his arm.

'Of course I do.' It was partially true, Joan believed, on Brandt's part, but not on hers.

'I never met anyone as coldly analytical as you are.' Brandt shook his head grimly, blue sapphire chips gleaming at her angrily before they sliced away and he rolled to his feet. 'You just turn your emotions on and off at will, don't you?'

Sheer nerve was the only thing keeping Joan from turning into a blubbering mass of tears. 'Don't you, Mr Lyon?' she challenged. The furnace had kicked on, sending warm draughts of air shooting through the room. 'You hired me because I was efficient, practical and not subject to panic at the unforeseen. Are you about to fire me for the same reasons?'

She almost wished he would. In fact she prayed that he would, so she wouldn't have to face him day after day, remembering always those moments when he had made love to her.

'No, Miss Somers.' There was sarcastic inflection on the impersonal term of address as Brandt remained turned away from her. 'I am not going to fire you.'

The moment of immobility had passed and his long strides ate up the distance between himself and the connecting door. Joan intuitively knew he was ending the conversation to assume his former sleeping place in the chair in her office. The bitter forces of revenge made her lash out at him one more time.

'Would you turn off the light when you leave? I want to get some sleep.' It was a request that bordered on a command.

Brandt halted stiffly by the door before reaching out to viciously flick off the light switch. Then the door was jerked open and he was in her office, violently slamming the door behind him.

Darkness enveloped the room. Joan wanted to curl up in the black shroud and die. Instead she huddled deeper into her coat, letting the tears of misery, shame and heartbreak drench her face. The silent release could not assuage the terrible ache. Nothing could.

Neither of them was truly to blame. Both had played an equal role for different reasons. Yet Brandt's cardinal rule had been broken. The line between his business and personal life had been crossed. The involvement of the two had occurred and it wouldn't be forgotten.

Joan couldn't forget. She loved him. Foolishly, impractically, futilely, she loved him.

CHAPTER FIVE

THE clouds outside were grey, not the slate-grey that held snow, but the oyster-grey of high overcast. The wind had subsided to a baby's breath that sent the top snowflakes dancing and swirling over the drifts piled by the harsh north wind.

The shimmering gold of Joan's long hair was subdued to a dull shade by its return to the severe bun at the nape of her neck. Her glasses were set primly on the bridge of her nose, more to conceal the telltale redness of tears and the blue shadows of sleeplessness than to improve her vision.

A soapy wash in warm water had restored much of her courage, but not a sufficient amount to allow her to meet Brandt's face squarely when she walked into her office from the outer corridor. Fortunately she didn't have to as his gaze flicked briefly over her with blue remoteness.

'The snowploughs are out clearing the streets,' Brandt told her, shrugging into his heavy sheepskin jacket. 'I'm going to shovel the car free.'

An acknowledgement of some type seemed necessary, so Joan issued a crisp 'All right.' As she walked towards her desk, he walked into the hallway.

Only yesterday morning, Brandt had thoughtfully provided breakfast and persuaded her to leave her hair down and curling about her shoulders. His teasing cajolery and attentiveness were gone and Joan wanted to cry at the loss. But tears wouldn't ease the desolation, as had been proved last night. The fault was hers. She should not have let his virile masculinity swamp her common sense. She had known of her feelings towards him and should have guarded more completely against him, but his warm, friendly attitude had melted her defences.

Brandt had said he wasn't going to fire her. But wouldn't it be best for her to hand in her resignation? Or would it be construed as an admission on her part that what had happened had gone deeper than what she had led him to believe? The answer seemed to lie in whether she had the strength to meet him in the daily routine of the office without letting him discover the depth of her emotion. After a few months, she could resign in favour of a better job offer somewhere. It would be suicide to stay working for him for ever, knowing the way she felt.

'Damn!' she whispered, clenching her hands into tight fists on the desk top. The problem would be in surviving those pride-saving weeks.

Then she got hold of herself. These constant recriminations over her actions had to stop. To keep reliving those painful moments after the electricity had been restored was serving no purpose. She had no idea how long Brandt would be gone, but she had to occupy her mind with something other than thoughts of him. She pulled the plastic cover off the typewriter and began typing the letters Brandt had dictated the first night. She was barely through the third letter when he walked into the office.

'Are you ready?' His quiet, calm voice stopped her fingers for a split second before they continued their flight across the keys.

'I'll be finished in a moment,' she replied, not letting her gaze stray from the shorthand pad.

When the letter was finished and it and the carbon copy were placed with the other two, Brandt was beside the desk, handing her the fun-fur coat that had been in his office. Her already wounded nerves smarted at his eagerness to be rid of her, but a swift glance at his rugged, aquiline face revealed none of the impatience she had believed she would see. He stood silently by as she put the coat on, his hands thrust deep in the pockets of his own jacket, a withdrawn expression in his eyes.

He ushered her without haste to his car parked in front of the building, its motor still running. The coldly invigorating air made the warm interior seem stifling as Joan settled into the passenger seat.

'Where do you live?' Brandt slipped the car into gear and turned into the street.

Joan gave him the directions and leaned back in the seat. Her side vision gave her an unobstructed view of his hawklike profile, but she kept her gaze firmly to the front. In other circumstances, she might have enjoyed the white purity of the landscape that had transformed the city streets into a wintry wonderland. The snow was firmly packed in thin layers on patches of the street, making the driving still slightly treacherous in spite of the considerable efforts of the snowplough. The lean hands on the wheel were competent and experienced and the nearly two miles to Joan's apartment were without mishap.

The pavement leading to the front entrance of the old brick structure had not been cleared of snow. The untouched white drifts indicated that no one had as yet ventured out on this grey morning. Pushing open the car door, Joan silently wished that some premonition last Friday had warned her to wear snowboots. Wading through those drifts would not be pleasant.

Before the sole of her smart leather shoes had become buried in the snow, Brandt was out of the car and around to her side. She glanced at him in surprise, fully expecting him simply to drop her off to make her own way into the building. A gasp of shock was torn from her lips as he reached down and easily swung her into his arms.

The corners of his mouth turned in a humourless smile at her quick, 'Put me down!'

His long strides were already covering the short distance from the kerb to the apartment's entrance. 'There isn't any need for you to freeze your feet in the snow.'

'I'm too heavy,' Joan protested, but they had already reached the door and Brandt was setting her down at the same time that he swung the wooden door open.

'You're tall, but you're not heavy,' he stated

without any emotion as he turned his blank gaze on her.

Her pulse refused to settle back to its normal pace. Just when Joan had thought she had regained control of her senses, she had been cradled against that rock-hard chest and lost anew. He stood solemnly in front of her, blue eyes unreadable, the staircase to her second floor apartment behind him. She bent her head to conceal the swift rise of confusion.

'There isn't any need for you to come into the office until noon tomorrow,' he told her. An apartment door slammed on the floor above.

Joan stiffened, tossing her head back. 'I don't expect any special favours, Mr Lyon, simply because I had the misfortune of being stranded at work for most of the weekend,' she asserted coldly. 'I'll be in the office at eight tomorrow as usual.'

An eyebrow arched into a brown peak of unconcern. 'As you wish, Miss Somers. Good day.'

As the outside door closed behind him, too late Joan realised that she had offered not one word of thanks for the ride home. In spite of everything, Brandt was entitled to a measure of courtesy.

'Lord! Ice nearly dripped from your voice.' Kay's excitedly astonished voice sounded from the stairs. 'And after the way he carried you to the door, too!' At Joan's surprised glance at the be-robed figure on the steps, Kay answered the questioning gleam in her room-mate's eyes. 'I was watching from the window. He was so masterful about it.'

'He did it simply because I didn't have any

boots,' Joan said tersely, 'and the pavements weren't shovelled.'

Her assertion didn't erase the impish smile from Kay's mouth as Joan hurried past her up the steps. There was about to be a deluge of questions and she needed the diversion of movement to collect her wits after those shattering moments in Brandt's arms.

'Is the coffee on, Kay?' she asked as she pushed the door ajar and entered their apartment. 'I haven't had a cup since before the electricity went off Friday night.'

'The electricity went off!' Kay echoed, dashing towards the kitchenette section of the room while Joan pulled off her coat and stepped out of her shoes. 'I didn't know the electricity was off! At least, I heard it was off in some sections of the city, but I never guessed you were without it at the office. Heavens! The nights must have been awfully long!'

In the act of pouring Joan a cup of coffee, Kay spun around, her sparkling brown eyes widening and her mouth opening in surprised excitement.

'How did you ever keep warm? The furnace can't work without electricity to operate the thermostat. Did you and Mr Lyon have to huddle together to keep warm? Oh! Wouldn't that be something!' Kay rushed quickly to the couch with the coffee cup. 'Is that why you were so cold to him? Did he make a pass at you?'

Joan flushed involuntarily. 'Oh, Kay, really! In the first place, we both had our winter coats to keep us warm,' not exactly denying her room-

83

mate's assertion nor explaining that they had jointly used the coats together, 'and secondly ... Mr Lyon,' she had nearly called him Brandt, 'found a space heater in the equipment shed.'

Kay pulled a wry face. 'It's resourceful, but hardly romantic,' she sighed. 'I should have thought you would at least be calling each other by your first names after an entire weekend together.'

Joan's fingers curled around the cup before she quickly sat it on the table in front of the sofa. 'I feel absolutely grubby after wearing these clothes for nearly three days. I'm going to take a bath and clean up.'

She rose quickly to her feet, not wanting to confide in her friend and room-mate, nor to have Kay's interrogation go any farther.

Monday morning brought a return of the strictly business atmosphere between Joan and Brandt. His gaze didn't cut her with freezing contempt, nor was he ill-tempered with anger. He treated her the same indifferently friendly way he always had, which made it easier for Joan to fall into the same pattern, at least, for the most part.

The main topic of conversation through the entire company was the weekend storm, with everyone trading stories on where and how they had been trapped by the blizzard and the difficulties they had gone through before reaching their homes. Joan was grateful for the insulation of her private office, segregated from the rest of the employees. It saved her from relating her own tale without lying. Kay had mercifully agreed to keep silent about it, knowing full well how viciously the story would be twisted into some lurid account by the office gossips, and as far as Kay was concerned, without foundation.

It was nearly noon when Brandt ventured from his office to request certain folders from the filing cabinet. Joan had just handed them to him when Lyle Baines walked into her office, a cheery smile creasing his face.

'Sorry to be so late reporting in, Brandt, but the snowploughs didn't make it to my street until after ten this morning,' he explained. 'That was really a first-class blizzard. Hope the two of you made it home all right.'

After Brandt had nodded an initial greeting, he had opened the top folder to study its contents. At the conclusion of Lyle Baines's statement, he glanced up briefly, a dark glow of concentration in his eyes as he turned to re-enter his office.

'As a matter of fact, Miss Somers and I got marooned here until Sunday morning,' he replied idly.

'The devil you did!' Lyle Baines breathed in his astonishment. His rounded, speculating gaze immediately swung to Joan.

Her dismay that Brandt should absently blurt out what she had been at pains to keep secret was written in her expressive brown eyes. Lyle Baines was not a gossip, but Joan didn't doubt that the word would spread quickly through the grapevine.

Brandt paused in the doorway. 'Come into my office, Lyle. I had a chance to study the blueprints on the Parkwood Mall this weekend, and I want to go over them with you before you start putting the prices together.'

Joan swiftly retreated to her desk, avoiding the questing eyes of Lyle Baines as he slowly obeyed the quiet, authoritative voice of his boss. Only when the connecting door closed behind both of them did she let her shoulders slump.

It was not until the following day that Joan was exposed to the results of Brandt's slip. When she entered the canteen with Kay, there was instant silence as all eyes turned to her. Then there were whispers and muffled laughter. With difficulty, Joan maintained an outward air of composure, knowing that to react would give fuel to their speculations.

Naturally when Kay discovered the rumours, she was quite vocal in defence of her friend. Joan knew that Brandt never heard what was said about them. No one would dare to carry tales to the lion, including herself. She wanted to avoid any further humiliation at his hands.

During the week, the gossip died from lack of further nourishment to feed on. Joan was glad she had kept a cool silence through it all. Her attitude treated the snide comments with indifference.

When she was questioned directly by the few bold ones about how she and Brandt had passed the time, she responded that they had worked, and that was true. Her own efficient and professional demeanour added credibility to her statements.

By Friday afternoon, Joan was congratulating herself for getting through the week. Not that it had been easy, because it hadn't. Some moments had held sheer torment.

There had been times when Brandt's hand had accidentally brushed hers as they exchanged folders or other documents and she would feel the rush of warmth at his touch. Or moments when he would be signing letters she had typed and she would be able to study the thick, waving brown hair, the ends curling on the tanned column of his neck, and the strong, assured face that held the hard masculine mouth that had so devastatingly awakened her latent desire and love.

At a little past four o'clock on Friday afternoon, Joan began the filing and general clearing of the work on her desk in preparation for the weekend. Clearing the 'out' tray was a considerable task by itself. She only smiled absently when the payroll clerk stopped by her office with her weekly pay cheque.

Preoccupied with the items left to be done, Joan removed her bankbook from her handbag, slit open the envelope containing her cheque and started to slide it into the bankbook and replace both in her bag. The amount of the cheque seemed to jump out at her, freezing her with a start. It was nearly half as much again as it should have been.

For a moment she could only blink at it bewilderedly. Then a slow anger began to seethe. She had no doubt that Brandt had authorised it to appease his conscience. Paying her off would release him from the guilt he felt.

The fingers that gripped the cheque trembled with anger as Joan rose swiftly to her feet and stalked to the connecting door. Her sharp rap was answered immediately by Brandt's 'Come in'. His gaze darted at her for identification before it was returned to the papers in front of him.

'What is it, Miss Somers?'

Joan was too angry to speak and his uninterested voice didn't help soothe her growing temper. The squareness of her shoulders and the tilt of her chin were dictated by pride as she walked to his desk and placed the cheque in front of him on the desk top. He glanced at it and pushed it towards her absently, all without looking up.

'That's your cheque,' he said as if she had brought it for his verification.

'I know it's made out to me,' Joan responded tautly. 'But the amount is incorrect. I want you to call the accounts department and have another cheque made out for my usual salary.'

The barely disguised anger in her voice raised his head. There was an aloof, searching sweep of her face that noted the glittering fire in her usually velvet brown eyes.

'That is the correct amount.' His eyes narrowed as the line of her mouth tightened. 'However involuntarily, you did work overtime this last weekend.'

'I have no intention of accepting any money for last weekend, no matter what reason you dream up, Mr Lyon!' Quivers of rage laced the sharpness in her voice.

Brandt leaned back in his chair. 'I did not dream up a reason,' he responded evenly, but a polar coldness had crept into his eyes. 'The fact is you put in a considerable amount of hours Friday night and Saturday on company business. Had you done nothing, I would have paid you nothing. The additional money is a compensation for your work.'

If it had not been for her indomitable pride, Joan might have accepted his explanation. As it was, she couldn't and wouldn't.

'I don't believe you, and I won't accept money because you regret——'

'That will be enough.' His command stopped her outburst with the silent swiftness of a rapier. Only the slight tightening of the muscles in his jaw indicated that anything akin to anger might be aroused. 'If you don't wish to accept my explanation, that is your affair, but the cheque is yours in the amount stated. What you do with it is your business.'

'I'll show you what I'll do with it!' Joan declared stormily.

With surprising swiftness, she retrieved the cheque from his desk top and tore it into small pieces. Hot tears scalded her eyes as she pivoted sharply around and dashed to the door.

She was within inches of reaching it when she was caught by the arm and spun around. Uselessly Joan tried to struggle free of the iron grip on her wrist.

'My God, Joan!' Brandt ground out ominously. 'I'm tempted to make you tape that cheque back together!'

Her head reared back so he could see the glitter of battle in her eyes. She caught her breath at the sudden clamouring of her senses at his disturbing nearness, intimidated by his height and breadth that so effectively dwarfed her. An angry exasperation was carved in his blatantly masculine features.

She grasped tightly at her own proud anger. 'It wouldn't do you any good. I'd simply tear the cheque up again.'

'I am not going to pretend that I don't realise you think the extra money is some form of appeasement for what happened between us on Saturday night.' Brandt watched the quick rise of colour in her cheeks. 'I've long since discarded the notion that I needed to apologise for what happened. I found you desirable and reacted accordingly. You were as willing as I.'

Joan couldn't meet his gaze. 'Then don't make me feel cheap by forcing the additional money on me,' she replied in a choked voice.

'I told you,' Brandt responded forcefully, 'it is for secretarial services rendered after normal working hours. I am not accustomed to paying for sexual pleasures.'

Her lips pressed tightly together to halt the outcry of shame. The high colour that had been in her cheeks was washed swiftly away, leaving her unnaturally pale.

'That was uncalled for,' he sighed. 'I apologise for that, Joan.'

'Please.' Her hand wavered weakly between them to ward off any more cutting remarks. 'C-call the accounts department and have m-my normal cheque made out.'

His grip on her wrist slackened to a less punishing hold, but Brandt didn't release her. Instead he turned back towards his desk, nearly dragging her with him.

'I will call the accounts department,' he agreed smoothly as he stopped by the chair in front of his desk and motioned for Joan to sit down.

The nearly abrupt withdrawal of his hand drained her strength, her limbs trembling beneath her. Joan sank willingly into the chair, surprised by his unexpected capitulation to her wishes. Brandt Lyon was not a man to give in once he had taken a stand. Conscious of her quick heartbeats, she watched him dial the inter-office numbers of the accounts and wages department.

His bland gaze flicked over her as if to make sure she was still there before he spoke into the phone. 'Connelly? Brandt Lyon here,' he said in his quietly authoritative voice. 'Miss Somers inadvertently destroyed her salary cheque. Would you draw another for her and bring it in for my signature?'

There was a pause during which Brandt looked at Joan, who was holding her breath under his pinning gaze. 'In exactly the same amount as before,' he added firmly.

Resentment flared immediately as Joan realised he had tricked her into believing he had agreed to her request. She bounded to her feet and raced from the room, flagrantly disobeying his order to come back. She didn't waste any time straightening her desk as she grabbed for her purse and dashed to the stand where her coat was hanging. Her hand was reaching for the doorknob to the outer hallway when Brandt appeared in the inner office doorway.

'Joan, you get back in here!' he demanded curtly.

She flashed him a fiery glance. 'I'm leaving early today. Don't forget to dock me on next week's paycheque.' With her sarcastic rejoinder ringing in the air, she stepped into the hallway, slamming the door behind her.

Although secure in the knowledge that Brandt wasn't about to chase her through the hallways, Joan still hurried her steps to the front door. She cast one apprehensive glance behind her as she walked quickly out of the building. Except for the curious receptionist, there was no one about. She arrived at the bus stop just as her bus pulled to the kerb and she quickly hopped aboard.

Kay arrived at their apartment more than an hour and a half later, stopping on her way home to cash her pay-cheque and pick up a trouser suit on which she had left a deposit. Therefore she was not at all surprised to find Joan in the apartment ahead of her.

'T.G.I.F.—Thank goodness it's Friday,' Kay translated as she flung herself and her packages on to the couch. 'Although I don't really know why I feel this sensation of relief. John is going to be here in an hour to take me to the movies and I have to be up bright and early in the morning so he and I can pick up Ed at the airport. Are you going with us?'

'I thought I would,' Joan admitted, finding she could not summon much enthusiasm for Ed's arrival—something she had looked forward to until last weekend. She briskly turned away before Kay could see her hesitation and resumed setting the small dinette table for their evening meal. 'The goulash is warming on the stove. We can eat whenever you want.'

'Goulash!' Kay moaned. 'I wish we could afford steaks. I wish *John* could afford to take me out for steaks, but he can't, not yet.' She sighed and pushed her small frame into an upright position. 'Lead me to the goulash. I'll eat and then shower.'

For all her disparaging remarks, Kay did full justice to the goulash and green salad Joan had prepared. Never one to shirk her share of the housework, Kay helped with the clearing away of the dirty dishes, leaving the actual washing to Joan when she insisted she didn't mind.

After filling the sink with soapy water, Joan put the dishes in to soak while she straightened the front room. Kay was out of the shower and dressing by the time Joan got back to the sink to do the washing up. At the quick rap on the apartment door, Kay bounded from the bedroom.

'John's here already and I don't even have my hair combed!' she yelped frantically to Joan as she raced to the door.

'He won't mind waiting a few extra minutes,' Joan smiled over her shoulder before rinsing a plate off under the tap and stacking it in the draining rack.

She heard Kay open the door, but she didn't turn around until she heard her room-mate's breathless 'Oh, hello.' The door was ajar, but its wooden bulk blocked her view of their visitor, who was obviously not John.

'Is Miss Somers in?'

Joan's stomach churned at the sound of Brandt Lyon's voice. A crazy surge of heat rushed up her body, threatening to suffocate her with its warmth. She averted her attention to the bubbling dishwater in the sink as if to pretend that she hadn't heard his voice carrying across the small room.

'Yes, of course,' Kay answered, her voice still dazed with surprise. Hinges squeaked as the door was opened wider to admit him. 'Joan?'

The curiously confused voice forced Joan to turn around. Her mouth quirked nervously in a false smile of surprise at Brandt's presence. He seemed to dwarf the room, making it appear smaller than it was already.

'Mr Lyon, what are you doing here?' Her voice thinned to a quivering note as he failed to stop inside the door but continued across the room to stand in front of her. She was unable to sustain the gaze that was rampant with ironic amusement.

'As if you didn't know,' Brandt murmured for her ears alone.

Joan flushed uncomfortably and darted a quick look at Kay. The small brunette had been watching them in stunned silence, but at Joan's glance, she hastily retreated to the bedroom. The closing door only increased the sensation of intimacy, and Joan wished she could call Kay back. She turned to the sink, deliberately immersing her hands in the water to hide their trembling.

Brandt moved quietly to the cabinets, resting an elbow on the draining board as he leaned back, effectively filling her side vision. His gaze seemed locked on the pulsing vein in her neck that betrayed her intense awareness of him. Joan started as his hand raised, only to flush guiltily as it moved into the inner pocket of the expensive suit jacket he was wearing.

'You forgot your cheque this afternoon.' The amused inflection of his voice mocked her as he set an envelope on the draining board beside the sink.

Joan swallowed. 'Is it made out correctly?'

'Yes,' Brandt responded with infuriating calm, 'It's made out correctly.'

'You know very well what I mean,' accused Joan sharply, but in an undertone.

In that lazy withdrawn way of his, Brandt studied her profile, lingering over each feature. 'After three years of working for me, Joan, you should know that I always have my own way.'

'Not in this.' Stubbornly she tilted her chin to a forceful angle that accented the graceful curve of her throat.

The lines around his mouth deepened with thinning patience. 'Why can't you accept the cheque instead of making an issue of it?'

There was another knock on the door and Joan quickly turned away from Brandt, self-consciously wiping her hands on her levis. She didn't care that Kay was already emerging from the bedroom to answer it. She needed a few moments respite from Brandt's unnerving presence, however brief.

Her eyes pleaded with Kay not to rush off with John, but John, for once, had his own ideas and insisted that they leave immediately so they wouldn't miss the beginning of the film. Brandt didn't miss her agitation when Kay and John left and they were alone.

During the interim in which Joan had studiously focused her attention on John and Kay, Brandt had removed his outer coat. The physical impact of his darkly elegant looks stole her breath. His evening finery made it difficult to associate the stranger before her with the man she worked with daily.

'Aren't you going out this evening?' he inquired idly.

His question struck a raw nerve. 'Isn't it obvious?' Joan looked pointedly at the cast-off sweatshirt of her brother's, then tugged the bottom over the hips of her snug-fitting levis. She felt gauche and ill-dressed beside him. 'I'm hardly dressed for a date.'

'With some girls now, it's hard to tell. There's a decided lack of pride in appearance – in public, that is,' Brandt added, an eyebrow quirking as if to indicate that he was not disapproving of the way Joan dressed in the privacy of her apartment.

But his criticism smarted just the same. 'I'm sure your dates are as impeccably dressed as you are,' she retorted.

Brandt was no longer leaning against the counter, but standing a few feet away. Joan brushed past him to return to the pots sitting beside the sink.

'Who's the lucky girl tonight? The blonde china doll I saw you with a few weeks ago?' she inquired with a decidedly cutting edge to her voice.

'You have the advantage.' His head went back, a sardonic light glittering in his eyes. 'You must be referring to Angela, because I can think of no one else who could be so aptly linked to a china doll. Unfortunately I didn't see you.'

'Hardly unfortunate,' she flashed, 'since you don't believe in mixing business with pleasure.'

His face was suddenly grim and she knew she had overstepped her bounds. Her hand brushed a strand of burnished gold hair back to where the rest was secured by a clasp.

'I spoke out of turn,' she shrugged defensively even as she apologised. 'Don't let me keep you. You must be anxious to meet your date.'

'I'm not so easily distracted from the reason for my presence in your apartment, Joan,' Brandt stated, his gaze narrowing on her face. 'What are you going to do with the cheque?'

'I suppose I'll have to accept it,' Joan agreed grudgingly.

He crossed the few paces that separated them. She wanted to turn away, but like a butterfly under a pin, she couldn't wiggle free of his compelling gaze.

'Do I have your word on that?' Brandt demanded quietly.

For a mutinous moment, Joan nearly didn't give it. She guessed he wouldn't leave until he got her promise. And as much as it hurt to have him so near, she wanted him to stay.

'You have my promise I won't tear it up again.' Joan tore the words through the constricted muscles in her throat.

'Nor stick it in some forgotten corner?' His

mouth quirked at one corner at the possible qualification of her promise.

'I'm not that wealthy that I don't need every dime I earn. I can assure you I'll spend it.' She glared at him resentfully.

Brandt smiled. 'That wasn't so hard.'

'You gave me no choice but to agree,' she answered, fighting that sudden leap of her pulse at the magic smile. 'How else would I get you to leave?'

'Are you so anxious to have me go?' he mocked, watching the way she nervously moistened her lips.

'Just as anxious as you are to leave,' she said firmly.

His gaze swept the room, then returned to her pale face. 'You never know. I might want to stay.'

'I can't believe you would want my unwilling company instead of the adoration of your Angela.' Waspish rejection coated her words.

His left hand imprisoned the back of her left wrist as Joan started to walk away. When she tried to pull free, the hold tightened and Brandt smoothly twisted her around and drew her to him. The incredible ease with which he subdued her struggles forcibly reminded her how very strong he was. That impression was soon erased by the electric tingling of her skin radiating through her body wherever she came in contact with him. A strange inertia took hold of her, reducing resistance to a vague thought.

'I can't get used to the fact that behind those glasses and ridiculous bun of my capable secretary,' Brandt mused on a curious note, 'is a sensitive and insecure woman.'

How badly she wanted his arms around her, protecting and soothing and stimulating. She hardly dared breathe for fear she would reveal the helpless hunger that assailed her. Tormented and aching with need, her brown eyes transfixed their velvet gaze on the knot of his tie.

With a savagely impatient movement, Brandt released her and walked swiftly to the chair where his overcoat lay. Inwardly Joan's senses reeled from the sudden shock of his withdrawal.

'I'll be late picking up Angela if I don't leave now,' he said sharply.

'It certainly wouldn't do to keep her waiting.' Her voice was sarcastically low and controlled to hide the quiver of pain.

'That's true,' Brandt sliced back. 'Unlike you, she's eager for my company.'

His supple strides carried him quickly to the door into the outer hall. As his hand closed over the doorknob, he hesitated and turned back. It cost Joan the earth to meet the compelling yet indifferent glare of blue.

'Will you be all right alone here in the apartment?' The question was asked with grudging concern.

Chilled, Joan hated his male arrogance. 'I'll be so buy tonight that I doubt I'll even notice I'm alone,' she declared coldly. 'Ed is flying in tomorrow morning and I have a lot to do before he arrives.'

His gaze raked her face. 'Lock and bolt the door when I leave,' he ordered.

Joan did.

CHAPTER SIX

THE filing drawer of the metal cabinet was slammed shut as Joan walked into her office. Her darting look was just in time to see Brandt glance at his watch.

'I'm five minutes early,' she informed him coldly, walking to the coat-stand to hang up her coat.

When she turned around, he was propped against the cabinet. The hard line of his mouth was pulled up at the corners in a mirthless smile while his gaze inspected her sardonically.

'I have never known you to be less than punctual, Miss Somers.' His arms were folded complacently in front of him. 'Although I did think you might cheat a bit this morning after what must have been a full weekend.'

In truth, it had been a wretchedly flat weekend. Too many forced smiles and laughs. Too much pretence that she was actually enjoying Ed's company or his kisses.

'Like you, Mr Lyon, I don't let my personal life affect my work,' Joan responded curtly. Walking to her desk, she removed her reading glasses from her bag and slipped them on to her nose. 'Now, what was it you wanted from the filing cabinet?'

'You've slipped back into your business skin,

haven't you, Joan?' The dryly rhetorical question mocked her subtle attempt to divert the conversation. 'My comment was motivated by a purely friendly interest that your weekend was all that you hoped it to be.'

'You're no more interested in hearing about my weekend with Ed than I am to learn the highlights of yours with Angela.'

There was altogether too much bitterly jealous truth in her stiff words. Her entire weekend had been haunted by visions of Brandt making love to the dainty blonde.

The carved features hardened. 'I want the completion schedule on the Blackwood project. Bring it into my office.' Then Brandt was pushing away from the cabinet and walking with long strides to the open doorway of his office. 'Let me know when the cold war is over,' he tossed back.

'I don't know what you're talking about,' Joan was stung to retort.

Brandt stopped in the doorway, his eyes narrowing as he met her haughtily cool look. 'I'm not accustomed to receiving a severe case of frostbite simply because I make a casual inquiry,' he snapped.

'We've never exchanged confidences in the past and I see no reason to begin now.' Her voice matched his own clipped tones.

'You sensitive little prig!' He laughed shortly and harshly. 'I intended no personal or private exchange. The type of conversation I had in mind was "How was your weekend?" to which you would reply "I had a good time." Then I would say

101

'"The fun is over and it's back to work for another week." My intentions were all very innocent!'

Joan flushed scarlet, firmly put in her place. 'I didn't know ... I didn't realise...' She fumbled for an apology. 'I misunderstood. I'm sorry.'

'As usual, you were making mountains out of molehills,' he stated dryly, the contempt leaving his voice. Her gaze skittered to his face and bounced away. His head tilted inquiringly to the side. 'Pax?'

Her mouth moved into a tentative smile. 'Pax,' she agreed weakly.

'Good,' he nodded abruptly, a dancing gleam suddenly appearing in his eyes. 'Then get me that completion schedule. It's back to work.'

Their truce was surprisingly solid. That infinitesimal tension no longer crackled in the air. True, it was bitter-sweet for Joan, but at least she didn't feel she had to guard every word on the chance that Brandt might misconstrue its meaning.

Besides, in this Christmas week, it seemed so wrong not to declare 'peace'. Christmas was a holiday of love, and her heart overflowed with love for Brandt. In another month she would hand in her notice and be for ever out of his life. It was better to leave a casual friend than the instigator of a cold war. He would be less apt to question her motives.

Her fingers paused on the keys of the typewriter, and she wished she hadn't reminded herself of her imminent departure. A minute before she had been rejoicing silently in the Christmas spirit. She was determined not to let herself sink back into the doldrums of despair. Tonight she was taking a bus home to be with her family on Christmas Day. She would not have her visit coloured with useless yearnings.

The door to her office opened and Kay floated into the room, looking like one of Santa's helpers with her pixie curls and bright red dress. A beaming smile of exasperation bowed her lips.

'Aren't you ready? Nearly everyone is in the canteen now, except you and Mr Lyon,' she scolded lightly.

Joan returned the smile indulgently. Kay was always the party-lover. The annual Christmas party at the office was one more reason to exhibit her outgoing and bubbly personality.

'As soon as I finish this letter I'll be done for the day,' she replied.

'You're much too earnest!' Kay sighed. 'What does it matter if that letter gets done today or not? Tomorrow is Christmas Day and it isn't going to get delivered to wherever it is that it's going.'

'It will only take me a few minutes to finish it and then I won't have it waiting for me when I come back,' Joan argued logically.

'Well, I'm not going to wait for you.' Kay wrinkled her nose and glided towards the door. 'The party is to start at one-thirty, and it's now one-thirty-five.'

'I'll be there shortly,' Joan promised.

When the letter was typed, she set it with the other stack awaiting Brandt's signature and cleared her desk. Kay's bright spirits were infectious. She found a smile came readily to her lips as she picked up the letters and walked to the connecting office door. She rapped lightly on the door and entered Brandt's office after his muffled summons.

He was leaning idly back in the large leather chair, a suggestion of a smile about his mouth that was disconcerting as Joan approached his desk.

'If you'll sign these letters,' she said, placing them on the empty desk top, 'I'll see that they get out yet today.'

'You're all done after this, aren't you?' He slipped the pen from its holder and began affixing his bold signature to the letters.

'Yes,' Joan agreed quietly, liking the way the pen flowed in concise strokes over the paper.

'You're late for the party,' Brandt commented, not glancing up.

'So are you.' A few days ago, before their truce, she wouldn't have been able to respond so lightly and naturally.

The last letter was signed, but instead of handing them to her, he began folding and inserting them in their respective, attached envelopes.

He glanced up at her and smiled. 'Yes, but the boss is supposed to arrive late and leave early, so I don't inhibit my employees.'

The smile sent shock waves through her system, and she transferred her attention back to the letters. 'I suppose it's only natural that we're self-conscious when you're around.'

Deliberately she placed herself with the rest of the company's employees, although she didn't exactly fit. Her closeness to the boss elevated her to some indefinable plateau.

'Are you self-conscious around me?' The letters were all sealed in their envelopes, but he kept them in his hand.

'Not as much as others who only see you from a distance,' Joan qualified.

His gaze roamed freely over her face and her slightly guarded expression. 'So to you, I'm not some omnipotent god with the sword of dismissal in my hand,' he mocked.

'You are my employer,' she dodged.

Her hand reached out for the letters. There was something omnipotent in his hold over her heart and senses, but she didn't liken him to a god. Almost reluctantly, he handed her the envelopes with their correspondence inside.

'I'll be off to the party now,' she stated, oddly feeling the warmth of his hands on the paper.

'Not yet.' An enigmatic expression in the carved, rugged planes of his face as he rose from his chair and walked around the desk to where she stood. Compellingly, his gaze held her confused brown eyes. 'There's something I want to give you first.'

'Give me?' Her echo was weak and barely audible as she watched him reach into his pocket and withdraw a flat jewel case.

Behind the patient and amused gleam in his eyes was something else that sent her pulse racing. Her hands were extremely unco-ordinated as they took the box from him. She could only stare dazedly at the familiar name of an expensive jewellery store scrolled across the top of the leather case.

'Open it,' Brandt commanded.

His eyes were on her bent head, watching, waiting. In compliance, Joan fumbled for a second with the catch, then snapped the lid open. A white-gold circle of linked ovals winked brightly at her from its bed of olive green velvet. Dangling from the bracelet was a rectangular object of the same shining metal in the shape of a filing cabinet. The drawer handles were diamond chips.

'I hope you like it,' Brandt prompted, twisting his head to the side to get a better angle at her face.

Joan pressed her lips tightly together, foolish tears of happiness filling her eyes. His gift touched her heart more than she wanted to admit. Since the very first day she had entered his office, the filing cabinet had been a private thing between them, sometimes the subject of disagreements when Brandt would misfile something in her absence or create an uproar when he was unable to fathom the system, but it had always subtly been there.

'It's perfect,' she assured him in a choked voice, trying to blink back the tears as she smiled tremulously at him. 'Thank you.'

A solitary tear slipped from her lashes. Brandt reached out and gently wiped it away with his thumb, letting his hand remain on the soft curve of her neck.

'You aren't going to misunderstand my motives for giving it to you, are you?' he mocked lightly. 'You're still receiving your regular Christmas bonus the same as everyone else who works for Lyon Construction. This gift is from Brandt Lyon to Joan Somers, with only the Christmas spirit involved.'

For a frightened moment, Joan thought he was warning her that the gift did not imply that his emotions were of a more serious nature. Then she realised he was referring to the scene she had made when he had paid her for the weekend they were stranded at the office.

'I understand,' she murmured, still with a catch in her voice. Her finger touched the smooth chain of the bracelet. 'From one friend to another.'

The lines around his mouth deepened into a wide smile, but something held the smile back from reaching his eyes. 'Let me help you put it on,' he said, and reached into the case for the bracelet.

Joan was beyond any protest as she offered her wrist to him. Deftly Brandt circled the bracelet around it and secured the clasp. Absently she wondered what a slave bracelet looked like, because he had just taken another portion of her heart and soul. Soon he would own all of her and she would never be free.

Staring down at the strong hand holding hers, she wondered if it would be so very bad to be one of Brandt's possessions, then flushed at her complete lack of pride. The silence had become unnerving and Brandt's eyes seemed to be probing too deep.

'I ... I suppose we'd better go to the party,' she suggested, then realised she had coupled them automatically.

'It's Christmas, a time for rejoicing,' he said cryptically. At her puzzled frown, his mouth slanted sideways in a smile that wasn't a smile. 'It's a time to let your hair down, Joan—literally. It's bad enough to have the boss around to spoil the fun, but a primly proper schoolmarm is really too much of a strain.'

Her hand flew defensively to the smoothly coiled bun at the back of her neck. His gaze raked the full length of her form in critical appraisal. With a smooth swiftness that didn't allow time for a protest, he turned her around and slipped the box jacket of her green and gold tweed suit from her shoulders, revealing her curved figure.

'What are you doing?' she asked in a breathless demand as the pressure of his hand brought her back around to face him.

For a brief minute, he ignored her question as his thoughtful look swept her figure again, minus the jacket. 'You're going to a party,' he said, and unfastened the top two buttons of her pale green silk blouse. 'You should look like a woman instead of a model secretary. Will you take your hair down or shall I?'

She didn't doubt for an instant that he would, and stepped quickly backwards to be out of his reach while her fingers fumbled with the pins in her hair. She couldn't understand why she was giving in so easily to his demands. Perhaps it was because her intuition told her there was nothing more behind his request than the reason he had stated, that and the fact that she was reluctant to argue with him.

'Much better.' His impersonal nod of approval was issued as the last hairpin was removed and the molten gold flowed down her back.

All Joan could see in his eyes was approval. There wasn't even a glint of admiration. What had she expected? For him to break into a speech of flowery compliments?

Yet, strangely disappointed, she turned away. 'I have a brush in my desk,' she murmured.

Her shaking limbs wouldn't carry her very fast. She had barely removed the hairbrush from the centre drawer of her desk when Brandt wandered into her office. His meandering pace carried him to the window where he remained, gazing silently outside, until he heard the desk drawer close.

'Are you ready?' he asked over his shoulder, hands clasped behind his back.

'Yes,' she agreed, then more swiftly, 'No.' Reaching into the side drawer of the desk, she self-consciously took out the small gift-wrapped package.

'A present for me?' Brandt guessed, tilting his head to an angle of amusement. 'From you?'

'From all of the employees.' A pale pink rosebud appeared in each cheek. 'I ... I didn't personally buy you a gift.'

'I didn't expect that you would.' The corners of his mouth twitched briefly upwards. 'If you had, I would probably have been very curious as to why you did.' His gaze flicked to the package in her hand. 'Did you pick it out?'

The red foil wrapping seemed to burn Joan's hand as she visualised the very expensive pen and pencil set inside. Considering the elegant bracelet around her wrist, she wished she had chosen something less impersonal.

'Yes,' she admitted softly.

'Then I'm sure it's a very proper and appropriate gift for a group of employees to give their boss.' Laughter lurked in the recesses of his low-pitched voice. 'Come on.' His long strides carried him to the front of her desk. 'It's time I put in my appearance.'

As she and Brandt entered the canteen, amateurishly decorated for the occasion, Joan was awkwardly aware of heads turning to stare. Brandt's hand, resting on the back of her waist, didn't ease her discomfort.

Several of the girls, besides Kay, had seen Joan after work and knew how truly attractive she could be. Among themselves they had often shaken their heads over her reasons for playing down her looks. The rest, including all the men employees, had never seen her in other than her self-imposed uniform. Their stares were more at her transformation than at seeing her arrive with the boss.

After the initial stillness, there was a general gravitation towards them. Brandt's hand remained in the vicinity of her back, leaving it to shake someone's hand only to glide back before Joan could slip away. Her vague feelings of embarrassment grew as more now speculating looks were cast her way. Unable to carry on inane conversations, she was reduced to quiet 'Merry Christmases' and hesitantly smiling nods of greeting.

She had completely forgotten the small package in her hand until one of the girls nudged her, saying, 'Give Mr Lyon the gift.'

Instead of delivering the little speech she was

supposed to give, Joan held out the package to Brandt and murmured almost inaudibly, 'This is from all of us at Lyon Construction. Merry Christmas.'

'I wondered how long you were all going to make me wait for my gift,' Brandt winked broadly to the group gathered around.

His hands were completely occupied with the bright foil wrapping and Joan used the opportunity to slip to the back of the group. Brandt seemed unaware of her departure and she wondered if he had really meant to keep her at his side or whether she had misinterpreted it.

The pleasure he expressed to the group when he opened the present sounded quite genuine, but with the tiny jingle of the bracelet around her wrist, she didn't experience any sensation of gladness. There was regret and a hint of inner sadness in her eyes as she gazed at the back of his head, slightly turned to give her a small view of his aquiline profile.

As if he knew where she was all the time, Brandt glanced over his shoulder. 'You picked this out, didn't you, Miss Somers?' he said as if he didn't already know. The people in front of her stepped to the side as he turned to face her. 'You have excellent taste.'

'I ... I hope you like it,' for want of any other reply.

'You'll have to remind me not to loan them out,' he smiled, complacently taking in her shattered composure at being the cynosure of everyone in the room.

'Of course,' her gaze not squarely meeting his.

A sudden light glittered wickedly in his eyes as he glanced above her head. 'I've never had a bolder invitation issued,' said Brandt dryly. 'I wouldn't be human if I turned it down.'

His curious statement bewildered Joan until she, too, glanced up. A ball of mistletoe was hanging from the light fixture on the ceiling. Her cheeks were stained crimson when she brought her chin sharply level. In the fleeting second of her look, Brandt had moved to her side. The room was agog with amused interest.

Helplessly Joan gazed into his bluntly carved face as her whispering plea broke the silence. 'Brandt, no——'

A taunting smile split the hard line of his mouth. 'Where's your Christmas spirit, Miss Somers?'

Her lashes fluttered down in dismay as his fingers closed over her chin. Her pulse thudded loudly in her ears, her heart rocketing away. Then the warmth of his mouth was firmly covering hers, taking more than a chaste kiss under a mistletoe and stretching the kiss out longer than was necessary. Due notice of those facts was registered by the spectators.

When the kiss was over, Joan reeled slightly towards him, but his hands were lightly on her shoulders, steadying her for the brief seconds until she regained control of her senses. Her eyes opened in embarrassed resentment as she met his watchful gaze.

'Ah, Miss Somers,' Brandt chuckled softly and

with decidedly hard mockery. 'I believe you would like to slap my face.' She would have liked to, if only to save her own pride. 'It was only an innocent Christmas kiss.'

The feelings he had aroused weren't innocent, but Joan couldn't say that. There was very little she could say, so she opted for the easiest.

'Merry Christmas, Mr Lyon,' inclining her head as she moved her mouth into a false smile.

Then Brandt turned to one of the men in his estimating staff, subtly distracting the attention from Joan. Kay appeared at her side, took one look at Joan's strained expression, and began some nonsensical chatter, maintaining the monologue until Joan was able to respond. Slowly Brandt filtered through the groups, ending up on the opposite end of the room from her. The distance wasn't great enough to remove her intense awareness of his presence.

It was as though she couldn't take an unrestricted breath until Brandt left the party nearly half an hour later. She would have preferred to leave immediately after he did, but circumstances dictated her remaining a discreet amount of time longer. Suspicion had surfaced again within the ranks of Lyon Construction that something was going on between Joan and Brandt.

At his departure, the eligible male employees began drifting to her side. Joan couldn't tell whether they were attracted by her looks or curious to find out if she really was the boss's private stock. None of them had ever appealed to her, and their slightly leering looks did not improve her opinion.

Tom Evers was the one whose advances were the most persistent. He gave the impression that Joan should be rejoicing that he was favouring her with his undivided attention. He was still clinging tenaciously to her side an hour later. She flashed a silent signal for help to Kay, who responded promptly, diverting him long enough for Joan to slip away.

Her bus would depart in an hour and a half for her home town. She would just have time to pick up her overnight case and gifts at her apartment and catch a taxi to the bus terminal. The last thing she wanted was for Tom Evers to offer her a ride. In order for him to accept her refusal, she would have to be blatantly rude. This was not the time to make an enemy of one of her fellow employees.

Her suit jacket Brandt had laid over the back of one of the straight chairs in her office. She quickly slipped it on and retrieved her bag from the desk drawer, taking a precious few seconds to get the correct change for the transit bus from her purse. As she started around the desk, Tom Evers appeared in the doorway. His stocky but well-muscled build blocked her escape.

'So this is where you ran off to,' he said, smiling at her suggestively. 'You could have told me you wanted to go somewhere alone. I know a more comfortable place than this.'

Joan hesitated for a fraction of a second, too aware of the length of empty hall that separated her office from the canteen. Then she walked determinedly to the coat-stand.

'I wasn't seeking a place to be alone. I'm

leaving,' she told him sharply. 'I'm spending Christmas with my parents and I have a bus to catch.'

He sidled closer. 'I'll give you a ride home.'

'No, thank you,' responded Joan firmly.

'Don't come on with that cold act with me,' he jeered.

Her eyes blazed for an angry second, but she swallowed the cutting retort and tried to step around him. Tom Evers had no intention of letting her get by.

'Don't I get a Christmas kiss, too?' he mocked.

If Joan had believed he would settle for one kiss, she would have gladly given him one just to get rid of him. But she knew he would interpret her agreement as a signal that she wanted more. His ego was simply too large.

'Let me pass.' There was cool hauteur in her order.

'You like to play hard to get, don't you? I don't mind.' Before she could guess his intentions, his hands shot out to grip her shoulders.

He was only a couple of inches taller than Joan, but decidedly stronger as he pulled her against him. She struggled desperately to get free, averting her face from his hot breath reeking with liquor.

'Let me go!'

Her angry cry had barely left her lips when the connecting office door burst open. Before she could gasp her relief at the sight of Brandt, he was pulling her free of the disgusting embrace and nearly bouncing Tom Evers off the wall in the process. The wind had not entirely been knocked out of

Evers's sails, and his malevolent gaze darted from Brandt to Joan.

'I didn't realise she carried your label, Mr Lyon,' he said softly as he straightened away from the wall.

'Get out, Evers!' Brandt ordered in an ominously low voice. 'Before I realise how dispensable you are!'

'It was a little innocent fun, that's all,' was Evers's parting shot as he walked stiffly out the door.

Quaking shivers chased themselves over Joan's skin and she wrapped her arms about her to ward off the chill. The memory of his hot breath was churning her stomach. The areas where he had touched her felt contaminated and dirty.

Fingers touched the flaming heat in her cheeks and she automatically pulled away from them. Then she realised it was Brandt standing in front of her. His broad chest seemed to offer such safety that she swayed against it without conscious direction.

'Are you all right, Joan?' His arms were lightly encircling her.

'Yes,' she breathed, feeling infinitely better in his comforting embrace.

Gently he smoothed the hair on her head. 'I should have known that suddenly producing the Cinderella in our midst would bring the lechers out of hiding.'

It was getting too comfortable in his arms. Her hands pushed lightly against his chest and Brandt let her stand free. She darted him a grateful glance.

'I'm all right now. Thank you.'

His mouth was pulled into a smile that didn't extend to the guarded, dark blue eyes. 'I was in my office. I couldn't help overhearing.'

'I'm glad you were,' breathed Joan, picking up the coat and handbag that she had dropped on the floor during her struggles.

'Do you have a bus to catch, or was that part of an excuse to get rid of Evers?' Brandt asked.

'No, I am going home for Christmas. My parents are expecting me.' She glanced at her watch. 'I have plenty of time to pick up my things at the apartment and make the bus.'

'It might be difficult to get a taxi.' His head was tilted to the side in an inquiring pose. 'I was just leaving myself. May I offer you a ride to the terminal?'

'I——' Joan was about to refuse, then perversely she found herself saying, 'Yes.'

The traffic was heavy, everyone rushing from one end of town to the other in the annual Christmas chaos of parties and family gatherings. Joan had only ten minutes to spare when they arrived at the terminal. Brandt accompanied her to the gate, arranging with a porter to take care of her luggage and packages.

'Merry Christmas, Joan,' he said, offering his hand in goodbye as the boarding call was issued.

'Merry Christmas, Brandt.'

She would have liked to linger a bit longer, but she knew she couldn't. Reluctantly she released his hand, tears filling her eyes as she lost herself in the throng of holiday travellers.

CHAPTER SEVEN

THE Christmas spent with her family had been one of blissful contentment. The traditional placing of the star on top of the tree on Christmas Eve had been saved until Joan arrived. Then her mother had paraded out the home-made eggnog, fudge, popcorn balls, and Christmas cookies for everyone to gorge themselves on. It had been a happy reunion with all of them staying up until well after midnight, laughing and talking and reminiscing.

Santa Claus still visited the Somers home. Even though the children were grown up, there was still a silly toy in their stockings on Christmas morning. Joan's father insisted that there would always be a little bit of a child in everyone and maintained Santa's mysterious night-time visit.

The best present of all had been when her older brother Keith had called from Germany on Christmas morning. Of course, there it had been Christmas afternoon. Only once had Joan allowed herself to wonder how Brandt was spending the holiday—probably, like her, with his parents.

With Christmas falling on a Wednesday, it was back to work on Thursday. Except for an offhand 'Did you enjoy your Christmas?', Brandt's manner was business as usual. Not truly as usual, Joan reconsidered, since he seemed bent on making up for that lost holiday time.

By late Friday afternoon, she felt as if she had worked an entire week in the span of two days. Yet she wasn't looking forward to the weekend. There would be too much idle time to think and she would rather work herself to exhaustion than bemoan the fate of unrequited love.

The loss of concentration had been brief, but it had only taken that minute's loss for Joan to invert the spelling of a word in the contract she was typing. With a tired sigh, she set about correcting the original and the three carbons behind it.

While she was correcting the third, the telephone rang. 'Brandt Lyon, please?' a sweetly low feminine voice requested.

Joan cradled the receiver under her chin as she continued her correction. 'I'm sorry, but Mr Lyon is in conference. May I have him return the call?'

'Are you his private secretary?'

'Yes, I am,' Joan confirmed.

'Perhaps you could help me,' the voice suggested. 'This is Angela Farr.' Joan's eraser froze on the paper. 'Brandt has tickets for a concert tomorrow evening. Would you know which performance they're for? My parents are anxious for Brandt to join us for dinner and I don't know whether it would be best to dine before or after the concert.'

The question and implication penetrated Joan's consciousness, but she was incapable to replying immediately. There was a cold deadening of her senses as she thought how aptly the delicately melodious voice matched the fragile blonde.

'I'm sorry, Miss Farr.' Her voice trembled slightly with envy and resentment. 'Mr Lyon handles any personal arrangements himself. I wouldn't have the information you want.'

There was a regretful sigh. 'Would you tell Brandt that I called and ask him to get in touch with me when he's free?'

'Of course,' agreed Joan tautly.

'He has my number, and thank you anyway.'

'Not at all.' It took all her willpower not to slam the receiver in the blonde's ear.

Joan didn't need anyone to explain that things were getting serious between Brandt and Angela if he had begun dining with her parents. Driven by an impotent frustration, she again attacked the contract in her typewriter and accidentally ripped a hole in the third carbon. Tearing the entire contract out of the carriage, she began again. She had it nearly completed when Brandt returned from the conference with his project superintendents.

'Do you have the Hadley contract ready?' were his first words.

'Almost,' Joan replied in her angrily tight voice.

Brandt frowned tiredly. 'I would have thought you'd have it finished by now.'

'I was interrupted by phone calls,' she told him curtly.

The messages were lying on her desk. Brandt picked them up, sifting through them. Joan saw him hesitate when he reached the note for him to call Angela.

His gaze swiftly caught her watchful look. 'Miss Farr called?' he questioned sharply.

'Twenty minutes ago,' Joan responded, trying to keep a professional crispness in her tone and not betray her stinging jealousy. 'She was anxious to learn for which concert performance you had tickets.'

Blue and probing, his gaze swept her controlled expression, then reverted brusquely to the messages in his hand as he turned to leave. 'Bring that Hadley contract in as soon as you're done.'

With only a third of a page to finish, Joan had the contract done, the copies separated and stapled within the space of a few minutes. She walked to the connecting door, and her hand turned the knob an instant before she started to knock. Brandt's voice reached her ears before the knock.

'Angela,' he was saying forcefully, 'I have to fly to Peoria tomorrow. Jake Lassiter, the engineer out of Springfield, Missouri, is meeting me there to go over the owner's changes on an interior room layout. If I could send someone else in my place, I would.'

Then there was a pause as Angela made some response to his statement. Discretion ordered Joan to close the door and wait until Brandt was off the telephone, but she disobeyed it.

'If I thought I could make it back in time, I wouldn't be cancelling our plans, would I?' he asked with a thin edge of exasperation. There was another pause. 'Your father is a businessman. I'm sure he'll understand.' ... 'Angela, I'm not going to argue with you. I have other calls to make. We'll discuss it tonight.'

Joan heard Brandt replace the telephone receiver on its cradle and rapped lightly on the door. When she entered his office, the receiver was again in his hand as he dialled another number. He glanced at the contract she placed on his desk and nodded a brisk approval.

'Craig Stevens, please. This is Brandt Lyon returning his call.'

And Joan closed the connecting door behind her, deriving no elation from the discovery that Brandt was not meeting Angela's parents tomorrow night, because he was still seeing her this evening.

Her entire weekend was painted a melancholy blue. Not even a bright sunshiny Monday could chase away the depressing shade. Brandt spent all Monday, Tuesday and Wednesday with Dwayne Reed of his estimating staff, going over the prices and cost estimates that had to be revised because of the changes of the Peoria job. Joan couldn't decide if she was happy or sad to see so little of him. With the strange twistings of her heart, it hurt as much not to see him as it did to see him.

Joan was lazing in a bathtub full of bubbles when Kay called out that she and John were leaving. Joan wished her a good time, then felt the silence seep into the apartment. Sighing heavily, she decided it was getting to be a habit to spend New Year's Eve alone.

Kay had suggested arranging a date for this evening with one of the men John worked with, but Joan had quickly vetoed the suggestion. For once, her room-mate had not pressed her to accept. Since the office party, she knew Kay had guessed part of what was happening. Yet she refused to cry on anyone's shoulder. People had fallen in love with the wrong person before and had got over it. She would too, in time.

The silence became pressing and Joan rinsed the bubbles from her skin and stepped out of the tub. After towelling briskly dry, she slipped into the olive green culotte robe that had been her parents' Christmas gift to her. In the combined kitchen, living and dining room, she switched on the small television set that was on loan from her brother while he was in Germany. Absently she didn't bother to change channels from the football game in progress. A noise to fill the silence was mostly what she wanted.

As she fixed a huge bowl of buttered popcorn in the small kitchenette, Joan wondered idly whether Brandt and Angela were celebrating the arrival of the New Year in private or at a party. The refrigerator door banged as she tried to shut out either picture from her mind. With a glass of Coke in one hand and the bowl of popcorn balanced in the other, she walked back to the couch in front of the television.

Propping a book in her lap, she had barely settled back against the cushions when she heard footsteps coming up the stairs. She smiled in sympathy for whoever it was that was spending the evening alone as she was. Then she thought wistfully that it might be someone's date. It was nearly nine o'clock, but some parties didn't start until late. It took her a full second to realise that the subsequent knock she heard was at her apartment door.

Frowning her bewilderment, she laid her book on the cushion beside her and padded in her bare feet to the door. She left the chain latch hooked and opened the door the few inches permitted to view her unexpected visitor. The world spun crazily for a moment.

'Brandt?' Blinking quickly to be sure she wasn't seeing things.

'May I come in?'

He didn't disappear and the voice matched. Joan fumbled with the latch, opening the door and stepping away, still expecting him to vanish at any minute. She had seen him in evening clothes and business suits but never dressed as casually as tonight. His overcoat was hooked on his finger and flung over his shoulder. The cashmere sweater of azure blue exactly matched his eyes, disturbingly studying her rounded gaze. Dark corduroy trousers emphasised the muscular leanness that his more formal attire had only hinted at.

'I saw the light in your apartment from the street, and wondered if you were home,' he said, stopping just inside and closing the door.

'Yes, I am,' Joan answered foolishly, since it was obvious that she was. She couldn't quite take it in that he was actually here. There had to be some logical reason. 'Is there some problem ... at the office?'

There was a strange brooding quality to his expression. 'No,' he responded, and slowly wandered past her to stand in front of the television. 'Is it a good game?'

'I ... I don't know.' It all seemed like a dream to

Joan. 'I just turned it on a couple of minutes ago.'

His gaze flickered remotely to her in recognition of her reply, then he tossed his coat over the back of the couch. 'Do you mind if I watch it with you?'

She had an absurd desire to laugh. 'No, I don't mind.' The words were barely out of her mouth when he was sitting down.

Her emotions muddled and confused, Joan uncertainly resumed her seat on the opposite end of the couch. Had he and Angela quarrelled? It seemed he would not show up at her apartment if they had not, yet she could think of no other explanation for his presence. Covertly she glanced at him through the veil of her lashes. He was staring at the television, virtually ignoring her.

'Would you like some popcorn and a Coke?' she offered belatedly.

Brandt seemed to rouse himself from some distant place. 'Yes, I would.' His gaze slid to her in acknowledgement for a brief instant.

'I'm sorry, but we don't have anything stronger in the house to drink.' The apology was offered as an afterthought when Joan realised that the refreshment of popcorn and Coke was more in the juvenile class than the sophisticated group he was accustomed to.

'I didn't expect you would.' His dry answer was raised to be heard over the television's sports announcer as Joan retrieved the ice cubes from the freezer section and another Coke from the regular part of the refrigerator.

When she returned to the couch with his glass of Coke, Brandt was already helping himself to the popcorn. His quiet thanks left her with little recourse except to seat herself again. He seemed disinclined to take part in idle conversation. She couldn't guess with any certainty whether his silence was due to his interest in the game or was brought on by some unknown happening prior to his arrival at her apartment. She was more inclined to think it was the latter. She tried to pretend an interest in the game, but her senses vibrated at Brandt's presence.

'Did you enjoy the visit with your family on Christmas?' he asked suddenly.

Her wits had scattered, and it took her a moment to gather them back. 'Yes, very much,' she answered, nervously plucking at the corners of the book beside her. 'My brother called from Germany on Christmas morning. I think that was the best present he could have given my mother.'

'Was this the first Christmas your family hasn't all been together?'

'Yes.' She glanced at him in surprise. 'How did you guess?'

'That fervent note in your voice. You were nearly as happy to hear his voice as your mother. You must be close to your brother,' Brandt observed, a suggestion of a smile in the otherwise expressionless face.

'I am,' she admitted. 'We always were except for a few years when Keith was entering his teens. Then girls, and especially sisters, weren't tolerated. It didn't last long, though.' She hesitated, unwilling to let the conversation die. 'I suppose you spent Christmas with your parents.'

'Yes. My sister Venetia wasn't able to make it home. She did telephone as well, but unfortunately before I arrived at my parents' home for the traditional family feed.'

'My mother made fudge and cookies and all that.' Joan leaned her head against the back of the couch. 'I probably gained five pounds in one day!'

'Wasn't Ed able to fly in for New Year's Eve?'

'No.' Joan hadn't asked Ed to come and he hadn't suggested it. In fact, he had made no firm commitment as to when he would be back.

'Still you chose to stay at home on New Year's Eve rather than celebrate with someone else.' It was a statement, but his brow quirked upwards in question.

'Not exactly. I had no other offers that I wanted to accept,' she answered truthfully. 'What about you? I would have thought you and Miss Farr would have plans for this evening.'

Brandt reached for a handful of popcorn, an enigmatic expression in his darting glance. She held her breath and waited for his reply, wondering if she should have asked, but somehow she just had to know why Brandt had come.

'Would you mind if we didn't discuss Angela tonight?' he asked.

So they had had an argument, Joan concluded, drawing a deep breath. 'I didn't particularly want to discuss her. I was merely curious why you were here instead of attending some party,' she explained rather than have Brandt think she was prying.

'I discovered I wanted your company.' His dark

127

blue gaze pinned hers. The lines around his mouth deepened into smiling grooves at the disbelieving look in her brown eyes. 'Don't look so surprised, Joan.'

'I can't help it. I am,' she swallowed tightly and averted her eyes with great effort.

He chuckled softly with a suggestion of hard mockery. 'If it isn't to see you, why else would I be here?'

There wasn't any other reason that Joan could think of, especially since it was plain that Brandt wasn't here to discuss business. So she made no response, her silence an effective reply.

Yet she couldn't shake off the feeling that an argument with Angela was the indirect reason for Brandt coming to her apartment. She didn't think she liked being used as a means of solace or revenge or whatever his true reason was.

The ensuing silence, broken by Brandt's or Joan's comments on the televised game, couldn't be classified as companionable. One seat cushion separated them, but for Joan's static nerves, that wasn't nearly enough. When the delayed newscast came on, she sat through the world and local news and the weather, but rose to her feet as the sports came on.

Her movement brought an immediate, questioning look from Brandt. 'I thought I'd wash the popcorn popper and butter pan,' she explained hastily. Glancing at his nearly empty glass, she added, 'Would you like some more Coke?'

'Please,' he nodded and handed her the glass.

While the dishwater was running in the sink, she

refilled his glass and carried it back to him, then returned to shut off the water, wishing she had a sinkful of dishes to wash instead of just a few. All too soon there was only the popcorn popper left. As Joan reached for it, Brandt had crossed the room with catlike quietness and was handing it to her. She nearly dropped it in surprise.

'I ... I thought you were on the couch,' she laughed shakily.

'Would you like some help?'

'No,' refused Joan self-consciously. 'This is the last.'

Brandt didn't return to the couch, but remained near the counter sink. Her hands trembled slightly under his watchful gaze as she thoroughly cleaned the popper.

'Have you lived here in this apartment long?' he asked.

'Nearly three years. Kay and I moved in shortly after I came to work for you. We both were living in furnished flats that neither of us could afford and that were much too far from work. When we saw this one advertised, we pooled our family's discards and moved in,' she answered with forced calm.

'When is—Kay getting married?'

'Oh, she,' Joan darted him a smile, 'is going to be the traditional June bride.'

'What are you going to do?'

'I expect I'll have to find another room-mate,' she replied as she rinsed the suds from the sink. 'Although I doubt if I'll find anyone as easy to live with as Kay.'

'Not even your boy-friend?' His mouth quirked in amusement at her look of indignant surprise. 'I was referring to marriage with this Ed fellow. Surely it's a possibility, isn't it?'

Joan swallowed the burst of outrage that sprang to her throat at her initial interpretation of his question. 'It's an unlikely one.'

'So he isn't Mr Right,' Brandt stated.

There was a trace of temper in her eyes as she turned to face him. 'Would you mind if we didn't discuss Ed?' deliberately using his wording when he had refused any conversation relating to Angela, and the bright gleam in his eyes indicated that he had noticed that.

With the dishes done and the sink cleaned, Joan would have returned to the couch, but his hand lightly touched the long sleeve of her robe, halting her as effectively as a high voltage wire.

'I like your robe. A Christmas gift?' A blue fire look burned the length of her body, sharply reminding her of her lack of attire beneath the warm olive velvet.

'From my parents,' she admitted with an odd, breathless note in her voice.

His hand fell away, but her breathing didn't return to normal. She directed her unwilling feet to the television and changed the channel away from the New Year's celebration to one carrying an old Humphrey Bogart movie. As she turned from the television, Brandt was standing there blocking her path to the couch, a serious, watchful look in his eyes.

'Do you want me to leave, Joan?'

Oh, God, she never wanted him to leave, she thought wildly. It was a totally unfair question.

Striving for an offhand answer, she replied, 'You're welcome to stay as long as you like.'

'You'd better rephrase that,' Brandt suggested dryly.

Her pulse jerked in her throat and a wave of heat swept over her cheeks. She swiftly lowered her gaze from the disturbing intensity of his.

'I only meant that you could stay for a while longer if you wanted to, but it doesn't place you under any obligation to do so,' she said stiffly.

'Don't be so enthusiastic,' he chided in a grim voice.

'Well, what do you want me to say?' Her demand was small and tight as she darted him a resentful look.

'It depends on who you're addressing the question to,' Brandt answered cryptically.

'I don't know what you mean.' Her eyes were directed anywhere but at his guardedly unmoving form.

'If you're asking the President of Lyon Construction, then his answer would be to leave now. On the other hand, Brandt Lyon would stay—for as long as you would allow. Now do you understand what I mean?' Brandt asked quietly.

'No. No, I don't know what you mean!' She shook her head angrily. 'You're talking in riddles, and I was never any good at solving riddles.'

She walked swiftly around him, afraid the confused state of her heart would have her read more into his words than he meant. His hand shot out to capture her wrist and pull her back to him.

'Then let me give you a clue,' he murmured.

His other hand slid beneath her long hair, tilting her head back to receive his kiss. A helpless victim of her love, Joan returned the hunger of his exploring mouth. The shooting fire in her veins made her boneless and malleable to the caress of his hands. She was without a self-directed thought as he released her mouth and drew her gently to the couch, where he cradled her across his lap.

Mesmerised by the unfathomable light in his eyes, Joan stared at him, breathlessly waiting for the touch of his mouth and not being disappointed when it possessively covered her lips. Her pride was forfeited. Physical desire hadn't destroyed her defences, but the golden flame of her love, that stretched to every sensitive nerve end, had.

Time was without measurement as she lay in his arms, pliant and responsive to his efforts to transcend the physical restrictions. The desire for total surrender mounted with each drum roll of her heart. The will to succumb to his unspoken demand for physical possession was strong to capture for all eternity the one moment in her life when she would be completely his. But the remembrance of his previous rejection was stronger.

Brandt's senses were drugged by the passions aroused. Her submission to his kisses had been too complete for him to guess that the reason for her movements was to be free of his arms. Her trembling limbs threatened not to support her as she stood beside the couch, her brown eyes misting with love as she turned away.

'I ... I'll fi-fix some coffee,' she stammered.

She never made it to the kitchen counter. The hands sliding firmly around her waist brought her to an abrupt stop. She inhaled sharply as Brandt buried his head in the side of her neck. Her fingers closed over his wrists, but she didn't attempt to remove his hands from her waist.

'I don't want coffee,' Brandt muttered huskily as his lips followed the route of her hammering pulse down the side of her neck. 'I don't want tea or Coke or any of that. All I want is to make love to you. Is that wrong?'

'Brandt,' she whispered. It wasn't a protest or an acceptance, but a strangely confused uncertainty that was partly 'yes' and partly 'no'.

The pressure of his hands turned her around, moulding her against the length of his body, ascertaining his need of her. Of their own volition, her hands slipped around his neck, the wild singing in her ears blocking out any other sound, and she was caught in the dangerous undertow of her love and swept along by the masterful tide of his kiss.

A key turned in the lock and the door was opened. A tiny, startled 'Oh!' was magnified a thousand times louder as it penetrated Joan's consciousness a second after Brandt.

Her hands were pulled from around his neck and she felt the ragged beating of his heart as her fingers trailed over his chest. She still hadn't guessed the cause of the sound, her tremulously happy gaze rushing to his face. The cold, nearly angry glare of his eyes was directed at the door. Joan turned in bewilderment.

A red-faced Kay and John looked back, poised just inside the door. Like a child caught playing with matches, Joan stepped hastily the rest of the way out of Brandt's embrace, her hands behind her back as if to hide the evidence.

'I'm sorry, Joan,' Kay murmured fervently. 'I didn't guess that—that anyone would be here.'

And most especially Brandt Lyon, Joan added silently, her cheeks flushing in scarlet embarrassment. She drew a shaky breath.

'It's all right,' she said aloud.

'Yes,' Brandt spoke crisply, a piercing look thrown at Joan, 'I was just leaving.'

His long strides carried him quickly to the couch where he picked up his overcoat to lend credence to his words. There was little else for Kay and John to do except to walk further into the apartment, silent apology still in Kay's eyes.

'Will you see me to the door, Joan?' Brandt inquired brusquely.

Joan hovered uncertainly for a split second. 'Yes, of course,' she breathed, self-consciously moving to his side.

Brandt didn't stop in the open doorway but continued into the hallway, reaching behind her to close the door. Incapable of meeting his discerning gaze, she stared at the carpet beneath her toes. The silence between them gnawed at her stomach. Brandt was several feet away, but she could feel his brooding eyes studying her.

'Will you come with me?' The quiet firmness of his request stopped her heart for an instant.

An outright refusal was called for, but she said, 'Where?'

He didn't answer immediately, waiting until Joan glanced up. 'To my apartment.' His calmness was unnerving.

'No.' She didn't trust herself to add more to her denial.

His sigh opened the wounds in her heart. 'Why?' he demanded quietly.

She turned completely away from his searching gaze. 'It was crazy for you to come here tonight.'

She couldn't answer his question. She couldn't explain that she didn't want to be the means by which he soothed the hurt Angela had evidently inflicted. And logically she knew that had been the only motive behind his kisses.

'Then why didn't you tell me to go?'

'How could I?' Joan asked with a bitter laughing sigh.

'By answering honestly when I asked earlier,' Brandt snapped impatiently.

The acid sting of tears burned her eyes as Joan forced the caustic words from her throat. 'How does a person go about ordering their boss to leave?'

'I thought you were different.' The lack of anger in his voice made his words all the more cutting. 'I thought there was a spark of humanity in you. But you're as greedy and self-centred as the rest.'

'Why? Because I didn't want to lose my job?' Joan fought back in helpless denial.

'Were you afraid of losing it, or did you see a means of keeping it?' Contempt lashed out.

'Don't ... don't try to place yourself so far above the rest of us,' Joan whispered. 'You were no better than I. Your motive for making love to me was to get back at Angela. I was a means of revenge.'

'What was I?' Brandt returned. 'A stand-in for Ed?'

Joan said nothing. Her heart was shattering into a thousand pieces like splintering glass. She could have suffered his indifference, but after tonight, Brandt would only regard her with loathing for the way he believed she had deceived him.

His hand gripped her shoulder and he turned her around, clasping her chin with a firm hold as his mouth punishingly covered hers for a white-hot moment. Then he released her, diamond blue chips cutting her to the quick.

'Happy New Year, Joan,' he said cynically, and he was striding down the hall to the stairs.

CHAPTER EIGHT

WHEN Joan returned to work after the New Year holiday, the air was so heavy that it could have been cut with a knife. On the surface, Brandt appeared as professionally businesslike as always, but his eyes held a suggestion of scorn whenever he glanced at her, which wasn't often. The whiplike flick of his gaze made tiny wounds in her thin skin.

At the end of the first day, Joan knew the situation was intolerable. There was no more reason to postpone her resignation. Brandt would undoubtedly be glad to see her leave.

Kay was more than sympathetic when Joan relayed her decision. The two girls had talked considerably over the holiday. Kay had bitterly opposed Joan's returning to work the second day of the new year. She insisted that there was no need for her to give Brandt notice after the despicable way he had used her to try to satisfy his physical desire. With her qualifications, she would have no difficulty in obtaining a new job elsewhere, and if she did, Kay assured her that with tight budgeting her salary would suffice for both of them.

Joan had remained adamant that she must give Brandt two weeks' notice, unless she was able to arrange for a suitable replacement in the meantime. Eventually Kay had accepted her decision, although she still believed that Joan was wrong.

Her intention was to type her letter of resignation as soon as she arrived at the office the next morning, but the instant she stepped into her office, there seemed to be a hundred and one things Brandt wanted done 'yesterday'. Joan hadn't a free moment until her lunch hour. Once it was typed and signed, she kept waiting for an opportunity to give it to him, but she had forgotten about his weekly meeting with the project superintendents. At leaving time, he was still in the conference room with them. Friday was as bad.

For the entire weekend, the resignation remained in her handbag. On Monday morning she entered the office with a fatalistic calm, determined that the first thing she was going to do was give the letter to Brandt. Taking the mail, the day's appointment book, and the all-important letter, she knocked on the connecting door and entered on his summons.

Brandt was on the telephone and motioned for her to sit down. She took a seat in front of his desk and shifted the letter to the top, wanting to get it over with the first thing. Her mind was going over all her well-rehearsed explanations, so she paid no attention to his telephone conversation. When he hung up, Joan took a deep breath in preparation for her speech, but she didn't have a chance to open her mouth.

'Is there anything important in the mail that has to be handled immediately?' Brandt demanded, already rising from his desk.

Her fingers closed over her letter. 'No, but——' she began.

'Cancel my appointments for today,' he interrupted, walking over to his coat. 'If you need me, I'll be at the Chalmers Street site.'

'What?' Joan murmured blankly, clutching the letter more tightly.

'That was Lang on the phone,' he replied, knowing that Joan knew Bob Lang was the project superintendent on that building site. 'There was a malfunction in one of the service lifts. It fell three stories to the basement and two of our workers are trapped inside.'

As she rose from her chair to follow Brandt out of the office, all thought of the letter in her hand vanished. 'Are they seriously hurt?'

'One is unconscious and the other man seems to have a broken leg.' He was shrugging into his coat as he opened the hallway door. 'I don't think I'll be back in the office today. Once we have the men freed, Bob and I will have to meet the safety inspectors. He's contacting them now.'

Only when Brandt was gone and Joan was back at her desk preparing to make the necessary calls to cancel his appointments did she remember that she still hadn't delivered her resignation. Fate seemed to be conspiring against her and she didn't want any more time to reconsider her decision. In no circumstances was she going to tear it up and prolong her agony.

On Tuesday Joan learned that one of the workers had suffered concussion and the other man had broken his leg. Brandt made a whirlwind visit to the office and headed back to the site. And the letter was still locked in her desk drawer.

Brandt was not in the office the following morning when Joan arrived. This constant waiting made her nerves all the more raw and tense. Again she placed the letter with the morning's mail and the appointment book in preparation for Brandt's arrival. She was on the telephone when he walked in. Her heart constricted sharply at the lines of tiredness etched in his strong face. He paused beside her desk, waiting until she was free.

'Bob Lang will be here in about ten minutes,' Brandt told her. 'I want Lyle Baines in my office when Bob and I go over the safety reports. Make sure he's available.'

'Mr Connelly is supposed to go over the accounts with you this morning,' Joan reminded him quickly.

'I've already put him off until this afternoon.' An impatient frown added to his preoccupied look. 'You get Baines.'

Joan picked up the receiver and dialled the extension number of his office while Brandt waited. From the corner of her eye, she saw him pick up the mail and appointment book with her letter of resignation sandwiched between the two.

As the ring sounded on the other end, Joan said quickly, 'I'll go over those with you in a minute.'

'That won't be necessary,' he responded, and walked to his office door.

At that moment, Lyle Baines answered the ring and Joan was unable to stop Brandt. She had always intended to hand him her resignation personally, not have him discover it with the morning mail. The instant she had passed on his message to Lyle Baines, she rose hastily from her chair to try to intercept the letter before Brandt found it. Fate was against her again as the telephone rang to call her back. Her nerves screamed in frustration as she jotted down the lengthy message while the intercom buzzed loudly at the same instant that Bob Lang walked in the door, followed within seconds by Lyle Baines.

Unwillingly, Joan flicked on the intercom switch. 'Mr Baines and Mr Lang are here to see you,' she said quickly.

'Tell them to come back in half an hour, then get in here!' The leashed anger in his voice came clearly over the speaker.

Both men had heard his order, so there was no need for Joan to repeat it. She accepted their silent nods of agreement with an uncomfortable smile, tension knotting her stomach as they left and she was forced to comply with Brandt's order to her.

The connecting door had barely closed behind her when Brandt spoke. This time his voice was briskly cool. 'I have an explanation coming, Joan.' The letter of resignation was pushed to the front of the desk towards her.

'I'm sorry.' Nervously she moistened her dry lips. 'I had intended to give it to you personally this morning.'

'It's dated last Thursday. Have you just now summoned up the courage to give it to me?'

Her chin tilted slightly. 'I would have given it to you on Thursday except you were in conference all afternoon and I didn't want to leave it for you to find when I was gone,' she explained crisply. 'And ever since, you've been very busy or actually out of the office.'

His finger tapped a corner of the letter impatiently. 'You failed to explain your reason for giving notice.'

Her gaze dropped to the desk, away from his penetrating look. Warmth began spreading over her face and she wished she had thought to put on her glasses to shield her eyes from his inspection.

'I thought it was obvious,' she murmured.

'Not to me it isn't,' Brandt returned smoothly.

'You can't expect me to stay working for you after—after——' Her initial outburst died away to an embarrassed whisper. Curling her fingers into impotent fists, she turned at a right angle away from the desk.

'After what?' he prompted.

'After the other night,' Joan finished tautly.

'Which night are you referring to?'

'You know very well that I mean New Year's Eve,' she burst out angrily at his deliberate obtuseness.

'As I recall,' Brandt leaned back in his chair with complacent ease, 'that night you were concerned about losing your job, and now you are intent on giving it up. Considering the lengths you were willing to go to keep it, you can understand my confusion now.'

'It's a woman's prerogative to change her mind,' Joan asserted.

'Do you have another job lined up?'

'I could not, in all conscience, seek another position before I had given notice to you,' she told him sharply.

'I suppose you'll want to use my name as a reference.' A thick brow arched in question.

'I believe my work has been satisfactory.' A flash of pride in the way she tossed her head.

'Above and beyond the call of duty,' Brandt smiled dryly.

'Would you stop making it sound as if I was the one who was cheap and disgusting?' Joan cried out bitterly at the implication behind his words.

'You were the one who allowed me to kiss you without making any protest, and not for the first time. Did you honestly expect me to ignore the invitation of your lips?' Again there was the mirthless smile while his gaze studied her intently.

'I ... I think you were mistaken,' she protested hesitantly.

'Was I? I believe I'm more experienced than you, Joan. I can tell the difference when a woman is being kissed or is kissing.' The razor edge of his tongue sliced at her as he leaned forward to pick up the letter. 'You've let your imagination run away with you, and I don't intend to lose a good secretary simply because you're foolish at times.'

'I've given you two weeks' notice,' Joan stated.

'Have you?' One corner of his mouth quirked. With slow deliberation, Brandt tore the letter into quarters and tossed it in the waste basket. 'I have no record of it.'

'I'll simply type another one.'

'I'm aware of your stubbornness,' Brandt agreed grimly, 'but I'm asking you to reconsider your decision. If you still feel the same way next week, we'll discuss it.'

'I won't change my mind,' Joan warned.

'You're very complex. I wonder if I'll ever understand you.' Then he sighed and bent over the set of official-looking documents spread on his desk. 'Get Lang and Baines in here.'

Joan never actually told Kay that Brandt hadn't exactly accepted her resignation. She had every intention of submitting another notice on Monday morning, so she told her room-mate that her two weeks' notice took effect on Monday week. Kay thought it was unfair and said so emphatically.

On Friday night, Kay began circling advertisements in the paper, insisting that there was no need for Joan to wait any longer. She should begin putting her applications in for other positions and Kay was determined that Joan would begin on Saturday morning.

There wasn't any plausible reason not to begin applications, but Joan didn't look forward to it, though she repeatedly told herself that a change of scene was the best idea and she should begin the transition as soon as possible.

Yet there was a strange mixture of relief when Ed Thomas arrived unexpectedly from Cleveland on Saturday morning and all of Kay's plans were set aside in favour of a weekend schedule that included Joan and Ed with her and John. Most of Saturday afternoon was spent in a friendly argument between the four of them as to where they would go for dinner and the evening's entertainment. Finally it ended in a wild compromise, that had Ed and John agreeing to cook an Italian dinner for all of them at the girls' apartment.

The incongruity of seeing the staid, quiet John in a frilly apron and his older, more aggressive brother Ed in a long bib apron from Joan's mother had both the girls laughing in near hysteria. The evening promised to be far from romantic, but to Joan, much more preferable.

Kay was rescuing the spaghetti noodles that Ed was trying to pour down the sink after nearly boiling them dry when there was a knock at the door.

'Don't tell me,' John moaned. 'It must be the apartment manager. He probably smelled the spaghetti burning and called the fire department!'

'Either that or he's coming to the rescue with a fire extinguisher,' Kay laughed, waving at the vague scent of a scorched something in the air.

'Or worse,' Joan said in a pseudo-whisper as she hurried to the door. 'It might be that lady that lives down the hall. She's probably outraged that we're "entertaining" men in our apartment and has called the police.'

There was a loud burst of laughter from the other three at that statement. Joan was doing her best to conceal a smile as she opened the door. Then all desire to smile was snatched from her chest as she stared at Brandt.

'Hello, Joan,' he said quietly, his gaze gently examining her face.

'Brandt? I——' Her head moved in a helpless protest.

'Who is it, love?' Ed's voice came ringing clearly between them.

The look in Brandt's eyes immediately hardened into something cold and withdrawn. Joan ignored Ed's question, knowing the door blocked Brandt from view.

'Did ... you want something?' she asked in a lowered voice.

A slight frown drew his brows together. 'I wanted to take you to dinner tonight.' His piercing gaze shifted from her face to the room behind her. 'I should have known when I couldn't reach you today that you were otherwise occupied.'

Joan stiffened. 'Why would you want to take me? Surely Angela had a prior claim on your company?'

His mouth tightened. 'There were some things I thought we should get straightened out. Obviously I was wrong.'

'What things?' she asked, desperately needing to know.

Brandt didn't answer as his bland gaze slowly studied her face, lingering for heart-stopping seconds on her parted lips. Her shoulders quivered lightly at the almost physical touch. He averted his gaze sharply, staring down the empty corridor outside the apartment.

'I wasn't going to invite you to my place, if that's what you're thinking,' he replied grimly.

'That's not fair,' Joan breathed. 'I didn't think that at all.'

'Didn't you?' he mocked harshly. 'Weren't you already questioning my motives, the way you always have?'

'Brandt——' His name was spoken in a beseeching plea for understanding.

She wanted to explain that she couldn't trust him because she cared so deeply and knew he didn't reciprocate the emotion. For her an innocent dinner in his company would be torturing bliss. None of the thoughts was expressed. At that instant an arm draped itself possessively around her shoulder.

'I'm sorry about the noise,' Ed was saying to Brandt. 'I'm sure Joan explained that we'll keep it down.' He saw Brandt's gaze shift with hard amusemeant to the pinafore apron Ed was wearing. 'My brother and I are playing chef tonight and I'm afraid we had a bit of a catastrophe in the kitchen which started most of the laughter.'

'Ed,' Joan touched his hand, realising that Brandt's air of authority had caused Ed to mistake him for the manager. 'This is my employer. Mr Lyon.'

'I'm sorry,' Ed smiled broadly at his own mistake. He took his arm from around Joan's shoulder and extended a hand to Brandt in greeting. 'I suppose it was a guilty conscience that made me think you were the manager. I'm Ed Thomas. Joan has told me a great deal about you, Mr Lyon.'

Joan had seen the thorough inspection Brandt had made of the man beside her. At the last statement, his cobalt blue eyes shifted to her, glittering with hard amusement.

'Has she?' he murmured, shaking Ed's hand courteously. 'Nothing complimentary, I imagine.'

There was a quick flow of colour into her face,

but Ed only laughed easily. 'Hardly. Joan has too strong a sense of loyalty. She has only spoken of you with respect and admiration.' His head tilted to the side in an inquiring manner as he glanced from Brandt to Joan. 'Was there some emergency problem?'

'There were a couple of questions I had to ask Miss Somers before Monday,' Brandt replied smoothly. 'I have my answers now, so please accept my apology for intruding on your evening.'

'That's quite all right,' Ed declared, magnanimously waving the apology aside. 'If you don't have another pressing engagement, why don't you join us in a glass of Chianti? The noodles were more ruined than we first thought and dinner has been set back for us. I'm sure Joan would like to have you stay, wouldn't you, Joan?'

There was little else she could do but nod agreement. Brandt hesitated for a moment, then shrugged.

'If Miss Somers has no objection, then I accept.'

When the apartment door closed behind the three of them, Kay called out from the kitchen side of the room, 'Did you pacify Mr Grady?' Then she glanced over her shoulder, her mouth opening in astonishment when she saw Brandt. It closed quickly, like a trap, at Ed's following statement.

'Joan and I have invited Mr Lyon to have a glass of Chianti with us,' he announced.

Bright flashing brown eyes darted a fiery look at Joan as Kay silently questioned her if she had lost her senses. Kay had never seen the need to hide her feelings and there was open disapproval in her voice and expression when she greeted Brandt. Even John's acknowledgement was stiffly reserved. Only Ed seemed unaware of the undercurrents of extreme tension in the room.

As Joan passed around the glasses of Italian wine that John had poured, she was vibrantly conscious of the indifferently cool blue eyes that followed her every move.

Their apartment was noticeably lacking in casual chairs. Brandt was seated in the rocker and Kay was perched on the footstool drawn over in front of the couch where John sat down. Ed was sitting on the opposite end of the sturdy Mediterranean sofa. The only vacant seat for Joan was the cushion beside Ed, unless she wanted to completely alienate herself from the group by sitting in one of the chrome dinette chairs. That would be an admission that Brandt's presence unnerved her, so she chose the couch.

Ed's arm was resting on the back of the cushions. The suggestion of contemptuous amusement was expressed in the slight curl of Brandt's lip. Joan realised that to Brandt, the arm so near her shoulders indicated a familiar intimacy that was totally untrue. She sensed that Brandt was deriving satisfaction from the taut lines of obvious discomfort around her mouth. She was terrified that he would deliberately linger over his wine to prolong her strain, but he finished his drink before the rest of them.

The smile pulling up the corners of his mouth looked quite friendly, but Joan had seen his true smile before and knew that this one was a bad imitation of what his genuinely warm smile was like. He thanked them all for their hospitality as he rose to his feet. She had half expected him to single her out to see him to the door when Brandt waved Ed back into his seat.

The only remark he addressed to her was 'Goodnight. Miss Somers. I'll see you on Monday morning,' delivered with a casualness that implied that his purpose for seeing her outside the office no longer existed.

The very day that Brandt had torn up her first letter of resignation, Joan had typed another. On Monday morning she was glad she hadn't waited because she found herself strangely reluctant to submit it to him. If she had left the retyping of her resignation until that morning, she probably would have invented reasons to postpone it.

Her resolve that she was doing the right thing hadn't wavered, but Brandt's unexplained visit to her apartment had raised questions of hope that she couldn't entirely shrug aside. Scolding herself for being foolish, Joan kept wishing that Ed hadn't been there when Brandt had come. She would have liked to have known what it was that Brandt had wanted to discuss with her. Now she had the feeling that she never would.

Although she hadn't seen Brandt, Joan knew he was in his office. There had been sounds of paper and footsteps inside the room when she arrived. Following their routine, she picked up the day's appointment book and the mail and a pad for any special notes. At the last minute. she included the envelope containing her resignation.

'What do I have scheduled this morning?' was Brandt's first utterance when she entered his office. There was no greeting, no alluding comment about the weekend or his visit.

In near record time, Brandt dictated what immediate replies were necessary from the morning's correspondence. His brusque manner invited no comment or query. That extreme air of remoteness made it difficult for Joan to find the words to bring up her resignation. In the end her courage deserted her and she rose to leave at his dismissal without submitting it. She was nearly to the door when Brandt halted her.

'Miss Somers,' he said curtly, not glancing up when she turned around. 'I'm prepared to accept your resignation whenever you have it typed. Contact our usual employment agency and have them submit a list of applicants and their references.'

'Yes, sir,' Joan murmured numbly. Her spirits sank as she realised she had been secretly hoping Brandt would try to persuade her to stay. Blindly she reached for the doorknob.

'And Miss Somers...' The sword-sharp gaze pinned her against the door. 'Please make it clear that this time I want someone older, preferably in her late thirties and married. Someone I can rely on not to be carried away by ridiculous flights of fanciful imagination.'

'Is that all?' she asked tightly, blinking back the tears.

'As soon as you've compiled a likely list of candidates from the applications, you can arrange interviews, hopefully for Thursday.'

'Yes, Mr Lyon.' The agreement had to be forced through the constricted muscles in her throat.

A brow arched in cold question at her tone. 'You are giving notice today, aren't you?' Brandt demanded smoothly.

Her trembling fingers sifted through the papers in her hand for the letter. As she withdrew it from the rest, her head lifted proudly. 'I hadn't changed my mind. I have my resignation right here.'

Brandt didn't glance at it when she placed it on his desk, but kept his studying gaze on her controlled expression. 'I know I can trust you to find an adequate replacement,' he said finally in dismissal.

Joan murmured a bitter thanks and fled the room, fighting back the waves of misery that threatened to engulf her. She had once told herself that Brandt would be glad to see her go, but she hadn't truly believed it until today.

After surviving that day, she felt she could survive anything, even the day when she would ultimately walk out of the office for the last time. That dubious triumph gave her the strength to return the next day, determined to carry out her duties without succumbing to the misery that dominated her heart.

Her mask of efficient practicality seemed to be firmly in place and unshakeable. Her voice hadn't trembled at all when the employment agency had called today for more specific information on their requirements.

She glanced at her watch. It was nearly eleven-thirty. Kay would be calling soon to go to lunch with her. Joan arched her back, stretching her tensed muscles as she drew the letter out of the typewriter and read it quickly over for errors she might have missed. The door to her office opened from the hall and she absently glanced up. She wasn't prepared for the vision of rose pink that floated into the room.

'They told me I could find Brandt here.' The china-perfect features curved into a charming smile.

From somewhere Joan found the ability to use her tongue. 'This is Mr Lyon's office,' she confirmed thickly. 'I'm his secretary.'

'Then you must be the one I talked to on the telephone a week or so ago.' The petite blonde glided softly to her desk. 'I'm Angela Farr. Brandt is supposed to lunch with me today.' Baby blue eyes glanced down at the diamond watch around her slender wrist. 'I'm early, but I hoped I could persuade him to leave now so we could have a longer time together.'

'There's someone with him at the moment,' Joan murmured, enviously noting the slender fingers and long. perfectly manicured nails that a typist couldn't possess. 'But I can let him know you're here.'

A conspiratorial smile flashed quickly, revealing pearl-white teeth. 'Maybe it will hurry up the appointment,' Angela suggested.

Joan's throat constricted painfully and she could only nod that it probably would be so. She pushed the intercom buzzer to Brandt's office, her palms perspiring with nervous agitation.

'What is it, Miss Somers?' a trace of impatience in the crisp voice that responded to her summons.

'Miss Farr is here to see you, Mr Lyon.' Her voice took on a frigidly cold tone in spite of her desire to sound indifferent.

There was the slightest pause before Brandt replied. 'Ask her to wait. I ... shouldn't be long.' His voice was distinctively warmer and it hurt.

As the connection between the two offices was broken, Joan glanced at the petitely perfect blonde. 'Would you like to take a seat, Miss Farr?'

'Thank you.' Angela sank gracefully into the straight chair beside Joan's desk. 'You're really very nice, Miss Somers. The way Brandt talks about you sometimes, I had the feeling you were much older.'

Joan was not sure that it was a compliment, but she decided it was only prejudice rearing its ugly head that made her want to read something else into the statement, if only to find fault with the woman. She would have preferred Angela to be a catty bitch instead of so openly friendly.

'Secretaries tend to be taken for granted,' was the only casual, noncommittal reply that came to her mind.

'Have you worked for Brandt long?'

Still unnecessarily shuffling papers on her desk, Joan smiled tightly, unwilling to tell this obvious paramour of Brandt's that she had handed in her notice.

'For three years,' she answered.

'You must know him fairly well,' Angela sighed, a whispering sound that sent the flowery fragrance delicately scenting her skin to fill Joan's nose.

'Not really, Miss Farr,' Joan denied, discovering she hated flowers, and most especially delicate pink rosebuds.

'Surely you travel with Brandt when he visits those noisy construction sites?' Rounded blue eyes looked at her, their largeness emphasised by naturally long curling lashes.

'Whatever gave you that idea, Miss Farr?' Joan laughed shortly.

'Well,' petite shoulders shrugged in confusion, 'don't you have to take notes or something when he's at these places?'

'If there are any special notes that Mr Lyon wants to make, he uses a tape recorder and I transcribe them when he returns,' Joan explained.

'I see,' Angela nodded. Then she glanced past Joan and smiled broadly. 'There you are, darling. I knew you wouldn't keep me waiting long.'

Joan's cheeks flamed as she involuntarily turned to the connecting door where Brandt was standing. The man with him, a salesman, nodded politely and left. Brandt's gaze flicked over Joan, then Angela, as if he were comparing the two. Joan knew who came out second best and she tried to convince herself that it didn't matter. But a tear slid down her cheek when the lean jungle lion walked out of the door with the delicate pink rosebud.

CHAPTER NINE

The sandwich Joan had eaten was caught somewhere between her throat and her stomach, a hard lump of bitterness and misery that refused to go away. It was one thing to silently wish for Brandt's happiness and it was another to see him with the girl who was providing it. Only a saint would be immune to the tearing pains of jealousy, Joan felt.

Her head pounded unmercifully as she tried not to glance at her watch. Resolutely she kept typing, concentrating on the words Brandt's voice was saying through the earpiece of the dictaphone, but her heart kept listening to the steady rhythm of his voice. Before she realised it, she had missed an entire sentence.

Frustrated and impatient and all too aware that Brandt's lunch hour was stretching out longer than she had ever known him to take, she replayed the missed part and didn't catch all of it again. With a defeated sigh, she turned the machine off and leaned back in her swivel chair, removing the earpiece and laying it beside the dictaphone. Perhaps if she relaxed for a moment, she would find the strength to hold her thoughts at bay.

The doorknob turned and Joan quickly bent over her typewriter, pretending a concentration on the words typed on the page as if seeking an error. She had heard those firm strides for three years. Unwillingly her gaze darted to her watch, a few minutes before two.

'Are there any messages, Miss Somers?' inquired Brandt.

Her head only half turned, deliberately not bringing him into her vision. 'They're on your desk, Mr Lyon,' she replied in a carefully controlled tone of professional indifference.

The footsteps paused somewhere near her desk and waited. The skin along the back of her neck tingled and Joan held her breath, her lashes fluttering down in a silent prayer for Brandt to be gone.

'Was there something else, Mr Lyon?' she asked coldly. Her mind was hatefully visualising the reasons why his lunch hour had lasted so long.

'Yes, Miss Somers, there is,' Brandt responded grimly. 'From now on, you wear your hair down. There isn't any need to keep up your masquerade as a Cinderella girl.'

Her pulse accelerated alarmingly as his statement caught her off guard. The desire to do anything to please him was strong, but he already controlled too much of her existence, however unknowingly. More share than a lion was entitled to. Her trembling fingers closed over a rubber and she began needlessly erasing a correctly spelled word.

'It is not a masquerade,' Joan retorted. 'I wear my hair this way because it's practical and I shall continue to do so.'

A gasping cry of surprise was ripped from her

throat as her chair was spun sharply around. Hands gripped each side of the chair, holding her prisoner in its seat as Brandt glowered threateningly above her.

'That was not a request!' he snapped. 'That was an order!'

The thick lenses of her glasses brought his face sharply into focus. She was stunned by the blazing anger flashing in every feature. Never once had she seen Brandt angry, not truly angry like this.

'No,' she murmured, uncertain whether it was a protest at his order or surprise that he was capable of such fury.

The tortoiseshell glasses were stripped from her face and tossed carelessly on the desk top before she could attempt to stop him. When she reached out to retrieve them, her shoulders were seized and she was hauled roughly to her feet. The lion was aroused and reacting with primitive violence.

'You will wear it down,' Brandt growled. 'And so help me, if you don't take it down, I will!'

Her fingers were trembling against his chest, placed there in case he tried to crush her against him. There was a wild ache in her stomach to disobey, to feel his fingers tearing through her hair and maybe even the savage punishment of his mouth on hers. But there would be too great a risk that she might betray her need to respond to his caress.

Hesitantly she raised her hands to the pins holding her hair in its neat, severe coil. Within seconds it was tumbling down her back and curling over the fingers digging into her arms. Bravely she lifted her gaze to Brandt's face.

The fury of his temper had subsided to a smouldering fire in the dark blue of his eyes. 'Are you satisfied?' she breathed tautly.

His mouth thinned. 'No.'

Her heart stopped as she sensed that the admission had been unwillingly given. His hands slid around her back, one moving to the back of her neck and the other to the back of her waist as he pulled her against him. With bruising possession, his mouth closed over hers. Joan quivered in resistance for an instant, then surrendered to her own hunger.

The door to her office opened and Brandt roughly pushed her an arm's length away. Lyle Baines was standing in the doorway, staring at them in open-mouthed surprise. Joan twisted her head sharply away, colouring in shame. Without uttering a word, Lyle Baines stepped back into the corridor and closed the door.

Not until they were alone did Brandt release his supporting hold on her shoulders. His fingers closed over her chin, forcibly raising it to look into his face.

'I have no excuse, Joan,' he said grimly, 'except that I wanted to hurt you. I never meant to succeed that way.'

Tears were brimming her eyes, but she met his searching gaze. 'From now on,' she said in a tortured whisper, 'save your caveman techniques for Angela. She might appreciate them.'

'If I thought beating you with a club would

help, I'd do it,' Brandt stated cryptically, and turned abruptly away, striding into his office as if, had he stayed, he would have tested the thought.

By Monday of the following week, every employee of Lyon Construction was aware that Joan was leaving and that her replacement was beginning that morning to learn the office routine under Joan's supervision. Everyone was also aware of the scene witnessed by Lyle Baines. The office grapevine was blazing with rumours and speculation as to Joan's true reason for leaving. There was nowhere in the building Joan could go without her ears burning.

Her replacement, Mrs Mason, was a small, greying woman with a ready smile. She gave the impression that with her varied experience she would catch on to the office routine quickly. Joan secretly hoped she would, thus enabling Joan to leave before the week was over.

Mrs Mason accompanied Joan when she went into Brandt's office the first thing on Monday morning to deal with the mail and appointments. Brandt appeared eager for Mrs Mason to learn quickly, as he addressed all of his questions and notations to her instead of Joan. Except for an initially brusque greeting, he ignored Joan almost completely, not even glancing in her direction. It was something of a relief when everything had been handled and she and Mrs Mason could leave.

'Would you stay a moment, Miss Somers?' Brandt requested calmly as Joan started to rise from her chair.

She glanced apprehensively at the older woman,

preferring the insulation of her company, but there was really no choice. 'Of course, Mr Lyon,' she agreed, and resumed her seat as Mrs Mason walked out of the office.

His expression was remotely bland when he directed his attention towards her, blue eyes reflecting none of his thoughts. An uncomfortable silence settled in the room, unbroken until Brandt pushed himself out of his chair and walked to the window, folding his hands behind his back.

'Have you heard the rumours circulating the office about us?' The question was tossed almost casually over his shoulder.

Joan blinked uncertainly, stunned that Brandt could have heard them. 'Yes,' she breathed.

Brandt half turned to look at her, a brow arching slightly. 'So you are aware that everyone believes you and I are having an affair.'

'Some have said that,' she agreed, lowering her gaze to the folded hands in her lap.

'Have you attempted to deny it?'

'There wasn't any point,' she replied nervously. 'I'll be gone at the end of this week and the stories will die naturally.'

Slowly Brandt turned around and walked back to his desk, stopping in front of her chair and half standing, half sitting against the edge of his desk.

'Do you know what conjecture has been made about your resignation?' His gaze was disturbingly concentrated on her.

Joan felt the heat spreading up from her neck. 'That we've quarrelled,' she answered.

His mouth twisted in a cynical smile. 'I think

that's putting it simply, Joan,' he mused with a tired sigh.

'Why do they say such terrible things?' Joan averted her head. speaking her thoughts aloud.

'Who knows?' he answered in taut exasperation. 'I suppose we gave them food for scandal when we were marooned at the office during that blizzard. It didn't help matters when I lost my temper the other day either. I'm sorry, Joan.'

'I ... I don't blame you, Brandt,' she said softly, rising to her feet in agitation and walking awkwardly to the window.

Brandt followed her, stopping beside her and staring out of the window. 'Will you reconsider your resignation?' he asked quietly.

'What?' she gasped softly, glancing sharply at his profile.

His level gaze darted to her briefly. 'It's the only way I know to put an end to these rumours. After a few months they'll see for themselves that it isn't true. If you leave, they'll assume they're right.'

It was difficult to breathe. His suggestion was so logical that she hardly dared to think about it. 'I ... I can't.' She shook her head. 'I'm leaving at the end of the week.'

'What would another few months matter?'

'Mrs Mason has already been hired to take my place,' Joan reasoned. 'We both know there isn't any truth to the stories and I won't let idle gossip change my mind.'

'The trouble is,' Brandt corrected, 'we both know there is some truth in what's being said, which is why the rest of it is all the more believable.'

'No!' Joan denied sharply.

'Have it your way,' he shrugged, and turned away. 'I thought I should tell you what was being said. But it's obvious you don't care.'

'Of course I care,' she protested.

'Not enough to do anything to stop it.'

Joan turned her head away from the cobalt gaze. 'I can't work for you any more. It's become impossible.'

'For three years you didn't find it so difficult,' he reminded her.

'But that was before——' She nearly said it was before she truly fell in love with him.

'Before what?' he chided mockingly. 'Before I tried to make love to you after you had invited me to do so? It isn't my fault that I never realised you weren't willing. I hadn't guessed you felt obliged to accept my caresses because I was your employer.'

Joan drew a sharp breath as pain stabbed at her heart. 'You only used me as a stand-in for Angela,' she accused.

'If I'd wanted Angela, I wouldn't have come to you,' he replied curtly.

Amazement mixed with confusion as she stared at him, wishing she could see behind his expressionless face and read the true meaning of what he had just said.

'Why did you come to see me New Year's Eve?' she murmured.

'I don't want to get into another argument with you, Joan. Let's forget the post-mortems.' Their discussion was closed. Joan could tell by the firm set of Brandt's jaw that they would discuss it no further. 'Mrs Mason probably has some questions. I suggest you go help her.'

'Yes,' she sighed, turning towards the door, then hesitating. 'I—I have an appointment for a job interview tomorrow at one. Would it be all right if I take my lunch hour then? Mrs Mason should be able to take care of the office by herself for an hour.'

'I don't care.' Brandt frowned and resumed his seat behind the desk. 'Make whatever arrangements that need to be made with her.'

The interview the next day went badly. Joan kept thinking of things she should have warned Mrs Mason about and had forgotten. Her interviewer had to repeat her questions several times. Joan didn't have to be told when she left the insurance office that she wasn't going to be considered for the position.

Her steps lagged as she walked down the corridor to her office. Before she reached the door, she could hear Brandt's voice carrying into the corridor.

'Haven't you found it yet, Mrs Mason?' he demanded, a heavy thread of exasperation in his voice. 'The man is on the telephone long-distance. What do I tell him? That we've lost his quotation?'

Was nothing going to go right today? Joan wondered silently as she pushed open the door, preparing herself for the worst. The frustrated expression on Mrs Mason's face turned to one of immediate relief at the sight of Joan.

'It's about time you came back,' Brandt sighed heavily. His own frustrated glare looked accusingly in her direction. 'Would you please show Mrs Mason where the folder is for the A. B. King Company? I have the man holding on a long-distance call.'

Fumbling through her purse, Joan removed her glasses case and slipped the tortoiseshell glasses on her nose. Her coat, she draped over a chair and walked quickly to the filing cabinet where Mrs Mason was hovering nervously and Brandt was waiting impatiently.

'I think I have the right drawer,' Mrs Mason said hesitantly. 'I checked the others, but I couldn't find it.'

Joan smiled a quick reassurance. 'This is the drawer the folder should be in,' she said, referring to the drawer that was opened. She flipped quickly through the folders in the 'K' section with no success. Darting Brandt a sharp glance, she asked, 'When did you have it last?'

'Friday. And it's not on my desk,' he retorted.

The corners of her mouth twitched in amusement as she directed her attention to the front of the drawer under the 'A'. There was the missing folder.

'Mr Lyon, if you would stay out of the filing cabinet,' she murmured with a rueful look, 'perhaps the folders wouldn't get misfiled. A word of warning, Mrs Mason, Mr Lyon tends to put folders in the wrong place. Whenever possible, keep him away from the filing cabinet if you want to avoid this kind of thing.'

'Thank you, Joan.' Brandt grimaced at her comment as he took the folder she handed him.

With the closing of his office door, Roberta Mason cast Joan a grateful look. 'Thank goodness you came back when you did,' she smiled. 'I knew you were so meticulous that it never occurred to me the folder might be misfiled. For a moment I thought Mr Lyon was going to tell me to find another job.'

'I wouldn't worry about that.' Joan walked over to hang up her coat. 'The filing system is one of Mr Lyon's pet peeves. As the old saying goes, forewarned is forearmed.'

'After today, you can be sure I'll remember that,' the older woman laughed.

'Did any other questions arise while I was gone?' Joan lightly touched the bracelet on her wrist. A wistful look crept into her face as she realised Brandt would no longer be turning to her to solve the puzzle of the files.

'No. Everything else went very smoothly,' Mrs Mason replied, then glanced at Joan hesitantly. 'May I ask you a personal question?'

Unconsciously Joan stiffened, wondering if the various rumours had reached her replacement. 'Surely.'

'I know you're looking for another job and I wondered why you're giving up this one.'

A guarded look spread over Joan's face. 'I suppose you've heard some of the stories that have been circulating,' she said coldly.

'Naturally,' Mrs Mason smiled broadly, her eyes twinkling. 'The gossips hope I'll give them an

166

inside track on what's going on. I had a notion to tell them if they wanted something for their malicious tongues to wag about, that they should look in their own cupboards.'

Joan tilted her head to one side in amazed disbelief. Her hair, worn down as Brandt had decreed, shimmered over one shoulder.

'Don't you believe what they're saying?' she asked cautiously.

'You're a very lovely girl. If Mr Lyon hasn't noticed that, I would think something would be wrong with him. Those nasty rumours are confined to only a few employees. No one else believes them, including myself.'

'Thank you,' Joan smiled gratefully. 'Sometimes I feel as if a scarlet "A" has been branded on me where I can't see it.'

'I assure you, there is none,' Mrs Mason smiled in return. 'But what made you decide to leave? Having been a secretary myself for nearly twenty years, I can tell that you're capable and efficient.'

'My reason is quite simple,' Joan shrugged. 'I've enjoyed working here, but I'd like a change of scene, to try something new.' Which was partially true.

'A new job is challenging,' the older woman agreed, apparently satisfied with Joan's answer. 'When you've worked at one place for so long, you seem to get into a rut.'

By Friday, Joan knew that there was nothing left to show Mrs Mason. The odd problems that might occur could not be second-guessed in advance and with Mrs Mason's experience, she would solve them without Joan's supervision. She was unnecessary, superfluous. She had been for much of the previous day.

Too much of her time had been spent gathering impressions of the office, storing up memories of the way it was. This last day was winging by too fast. Although she had been on two more job interviews, she still had not found a new position.

Last night Kay had suggested trying one of the agencies that provided temporary help when regular secretaries were on vacation or ill. It sounded the best solution. Her life already seemed to be in limbo and a constant variety of jobs and work locations might help her through the transition period. No matter how often she reminded herself that she was doing the right thing, Joan was reluctant to work for anyone else other than Brandt permanently.

During her lunch hour on Friday, there had been a small 'going away' party given by the rest of the employees. Mrs Mason's assertion that the rumours were believed to be true by only a few proved correct. The majority of the staff were sincerely sorry to see her leave. Brandt had arrived in the canteen just as Kay had been deputised to give her the gift that had been jointly given by everyone.

The most difficult thing had been accepting Brandt's expressions of regret at seeing her leave and his gratitude for the fine work she had done. Joan knew that his appearance had been motivated by a sense of duty. His little speech had been expected of him by the rest of the staff. She didn't doubt the sincerity of his compliments, but she didn't believe he was sorry to see her go.

As she walked with Kay out of the building that night for the last time, Joan pressed her lips tightly together and blinked at the tears burning her eyes. She couldn't help feeling sorry for herself.

'So help me, Joan,' Kay muttered beneath her breath. 'If you start crying, I'll brain you!'

Joan's short burst of laughter was caught back by a sob. 'It's stupid, isn't it? I couldn't bear to stay and I can't stand to leave.'

'I'd be handing in my notice, too, if it wasn't for the fact that I wouldn't be able to have paid vacation time when John and I go on our honeymoon. But I won't stay working here very long once we're married,' her room-mate declared.

'That reminds me,' Joan determinedly swallowed the tight lump in her throat. 'Brandt gave me my vacation pay, so I have two weeks' grace to get another job.'

'If he hadn't given it to you, you should have demanded it. After all, you were entitled to it.' Kay tossed her head, bridling automatically at the mention of Brandt's name.

Joan had never been able to make Kay understand that the fault for what had happened didn't rest with Brandt alone. She had contributed to their problems. She had worked with Brandt too long not to know he would never have attempted to make love to her if she hadn't indicated that she wanted him. But then friends were friends because they stood beside you no matter what.

'We're going to celebrate this weekend,' Kay

announced, refusing to let Joan's morose silence dominate them. 'The first thing we're going to do tonight is stop at the grocery store and buy some steaks. Tomorrow we'll go shopping and buy some outlandishly ridiculous clothes. Doesn't that sound like a great idea?'

'I thought buying hats was the way to forget your problems,' Joan teased to hide her lack of enthusiasm.

'Who wears hats except at Easter?' Kay shrugged as their bus pulled up to the kerb. 'Besides, I stopped at this crazy little second-hand store last week and they have some terrific clothes.'

As long as Kay was around, Joan knew she would never be allowed time to be miserable. It was frightening to think what it would be like when Kay was married and gone six months from now. Suddenly she wondered if she herself would ever get married. Without trying to make herself out as a martyr, she somehow doubted it. Before she had ever met Brandt, she had spent most of her weekends alone or in the company of other girls. After knowing Brandt and loving him, she didn't think she could settle for second-best.

'Joan!' Kay waved her hand in front of her face. 'I asked you twice what you wanted to eat with your steak.'

'I'm sorry. I was thinking,' Joan apologised, shaking her mind free of Brandt's image.

'And I know what about. Really, Joan, you have to forget him. Men like him aren't worth crying about,' her room-mate answered impatiently. 'Shall we have baked potatoes stuffed with Roquefort dressing and cheese? Or——'

But Joan had already let her thoughts drift back to the weekend when she and Brandt had shared less appetising meals together with a cold north wind raging outside and snow mounding the earth.

CHAPTER TEN

'YES, you are going to put it on now!' Kay declared, tearing open the sack and shaking out the floor-length robe of Oriental silk. 'What did you buy a lounging robe for if it wasn't to wear around the apartment?'

'I already have one that Mom and Dad gave me for Christmas,' Joan laughed. 'I don't know how I let you talk me into buying another.'

'You bought it just so I would shut up and you know it!' Kay wrinkled her nose with a mischievous smile. 'And you looked absolutely scrumptious in it. Besides, it was a steal at the price you paid.'

'It is beautiful,' Joan agreed as the sleek material slipped luxuriously through her fingers.

The brilliant golds and reds and blues had seemed to give her hair a richer shade when she had tried it on at the second-hand store where Kay had taken her. Wearing it, Joan had felt like some exotic flower. She secretly wished Brandt had seen her. But now, back in their unsophisticatedly furnished apartment, the robe didn't seem right for her.

'Go and try it on,' Kay ordered impatiently. She pushed the robe into Joan's hand and turned her towards the bedroom. 'And I'll get the tea made while you're changing.'

Kay was trying too hard to keep her in good spirits for Joan not to agree. The robe seemed to lose some of its magic as she slipped it over her head and stood in front of the dresser mirror. Or maybe it was just that some of the delight had gone out of her eyes when she wished Brandt had seen her. She tried smiling at her reflection, but the effect was a brittle movement of her mouth. Quickly she ran a brush over her golden hair, determined not to reveal her inner depression to Kay.

'So sorry don't have honourable fortune cookies,' the sing-song voice of her room-mate said as she bowed low when Joan walked into the room, drawing a more genuine smile. 'It will have to be vanilla wafers.'

The kettle began whistling merrily. 'Now, it's your turn to put on your gypsy outfit,' Joan returned. 'And when we finish our tea, you can read the teal-leaves to make up for forgetting to buy fortune cookies on your spending spree.'

'Wait until John sees me in that!' Kay laughed gaily, pausing by the couch to pick up her own package. She paused in the bedroom doorway. 'Can I borrow your gold chain necklace?'

'Sure. It's in my jewel box. Help yourself,' Joan nodded, reaching into the cupboard for the cups and saucers while the tea steeped in the hot water.

She was just pouring the tea into the cups when Kay whirled into the room, her bare feet skipping over the carpet. She stopped, posing in the centre of the room, the calf-length skirt swirling about her legs.

'What I really need is a long brunette wig,' Kay declared.

'You'd shock John to death,' Joan chuckled, carrying the cups to the coffee table in front of the couch. 'Where are you ever going to wear that outfit?'

'Who cares?' Kay shrugged, sinking lightly to the floor in front of the table in true gypsy fashion. There was an impish gleam in her pert brown eyes as she glanced at Joan. 'He's supposed to come over this afternoon for an hour. Do you really think it will shock him to see me dressed like this?'

'Well, maybe not shock,' Joan qualified. 'He's probably beginning to realise he can expect anything out of you, but I'm sure he'll be surprised.'

There was a knock at the door and Kay bounded to her feet. 'Good heavens! He's here already.'

She quickly smoothed her skirt and adjusted the elastic neckline of her blouse to a more daring angle. With a quick wink at Joan, she dashed to the door, swinging it open with a flourish. But instead of almost throwing herself in John's arms, she stopped inside the door.

'What do you want?' she demanded harshly, and Joan sat up straighter on the couch, stunned by the loathing in her friend's voice.

'Is Joan here?'

Her heart turned over at the rich, low sound of Brandt's voice. She rose quickly to her feet—whether to flee the room or run to the door, she didn't know as she waited like a statue beside the couch.

'If she was,' Kay was answering, 'she wouldn't want to see you.'

'Well, I would like to see her. Would you tell her I'm here?' Brandt responded. She sensed the patience in his tone, and the irritation, too.

'If it has to do with business,' Kay was still blocking the door, 'Mrs Mason is your secretary now. Go and find her.'

'It's Joan I want to see, not Mrs Mason.'

Joan knew that tone, the one that said Brandt would stand for no interference. Her fingers twisted together in agitation.

'Haven't you caused enough trouble, Mr Lyon?' her room-mate cried angrily. 'Why don't you leave her alone?'

'I understand your motives in trying to protect your friend,' Brandt said crisply, 'but I'm not leaving until I speak to Joan.'

'You're in for a long wait!' And Kay started to slam the door.

It moved only a few inches and it was stopped by a stronger force pushing it open. Nothing was going to deter Brandt. Drawing a deep breath to steady her shaking nerves, Joan stepped around the coffee table, accepting the inevitable.

'It's all right, Kay,' she said tremulously. 'I'll speak to him.'

An angry glance was flashed at her as Kay stayed mutinously in front of the doorway. 'You don't have to talk to him, Joan. We can call the police.

He doesn't own you any more. You don't have to do what he tells you.'

'Kay, please!' Joan murmured.

'You're a glutton for punishment!' Kay declared, and stalked away from the door to stand beside Joan, her arms crossed in front of her as if she was ready to do battle at a moment's notice.

Brandt walked into the small apartment, his hands shoved deep in the pockets of his coat. He stopped just inside, his diamond-sharp gaze riveted on Joan's pale face. Then it quickly swung to encompass the length of her, richly garbed in bright Oriental silk. She felt her legs quaking beneath her at the impassive expression on his compelling face.

It was barely twenty-four hours since she had last seen him. Yet that last time hadn't made near the physical impact on her system as she felt now—probably because she had convinced herself that she would never see him again. The wounds in her heart throbbed with pain.

'What do you want, Mr Lyon?' She had to force herself to speak.

'I want to speak to you. I thought I had made that clear.' His mouth curved cynically, adding to the harshness of his rugged features.

'There really isn't anything we have to talk about.' She couldn't meet his gaze any longer and lowered her own to her hands.

'I believe there is.'

'If it has to do with work, as Kay said, you should contact Mrs Mason.'

A disgusted sound of exasperation came from his

throat. 'I'm perfectly aware that you don't work for me any more, Joan. If you would ask your watchdog to leave the room, I will explain why I'm here.'

Joan glanced hesitantly at Kay, who was still glowering at Brandt. Frightened and vulnerable, she knew she should insist that whatever he had to tell her could be said in front of her friend. Kay was her crutch, her moral support. Without her, Joan might forget to obey her common sense.

'Kay,' her voice shook as her treacherous emotions took over, 'would you mind waiting in the bedroom?'

A bare foot stamped the carpet in anger and exasperation. For an instant Joan was positive Kay was going to refuse. Then blazing dark eyes tossed fire arrows at Brandt, a silent warning that she would be out of the bedroom like an avenging mother bird should he attempt to molest Joan. The full gypsy skirt whirled about her legs as Kay bounced from the room.

Joan's gaze was drawn back to Brandt, but it couldn't linger. She seemed incapable of looking at him without betraying the leap her heart made. Her fingers still were clenched in front of her, knuckles white where the skin was drawn tautly over bone. Brandt took a step forward and her gaze flew to him in alarm. The hard line of his mouth tightened in grimness as metallic blue eyes raked her form.

'That robe is very beautiful.' The comment was uttered with indifference, yet the compliment made Joan's lips tremble with gladness. Brandt withdrew its effect with his next words. 'Somehow it makes you look even more untouchable and aloof.'

Nervously she smoothed her hands over the silk, then let her fingers resume their curling knots. 'You didn't come to discuss my clothes,' she reminded him with a weak flash of pride.

There was a quick exhalation of disgust. 'Why are we no longer capable of idle conversation?' he wanted to know.

'We never were,' Joan murmured.

'Yes, we were,' Brandt sighed. Unbuttoning his coat, he gazed at her sharply. 'May I take my coat off, or will you regard it as some overt act against your person?'

The dry sarcasm in his voice sent her lashes fluttering down to conceal the anguish glittering in her eyes. The wavering movements of her hand signalled her permission. Her voice failed her.

'If you haven't turned into a statue, may I have some tea?'

The few steps had been taken to bring Brandt to the rocker where he had deposited his coat. Hard cold anger glittered in his eyes as Joan involuntarily flinched under the cutting edge of his question.

'Why?' Her brown eyes, wary and hurt, slid to him. It was dangerous to share anything with him.

'Because the air is cold and inhospitable, outside and in this room and I need something to warm me. Tea will do, unless you want to volunteer.' The quirk of his mouth was without warmth or humour.

Joan hastened to the kitchen where the teapot

was still warming on the stove. The cup clattered in the saucer as she tried to hold it steady and pour tea into it at the same time. Brandt was seated on the sofa. Joan ignored the vacant cushion beside him as she sat his cup on the coffee table and chose the safer distance of the rocking chair. Her action drew a glittering look of harsh amusement.

His hand was iron-steady as he picked up the cup. 'Have you found a job?'

'Not yet.' Her chin tilted a fraction of an inch to show it didn't matter.

'What type are you looking for? I know quite a few businessmen. I might be able to arrange to find you work.' He was settled lazily against the back of the couch, controlled and untouched by the tension that had Joan's nerves jumping.

'No, thank you,' she refused sharply. 'I would prefer not to be under any obligation to you, Mr Lyon.'

A muscle in his jaw twitched. His narrowed gaze swung from her face to the twisted hands in her lap. 'I see you're still wearing the bracelet.'

Her hand raced to cover it too late. 'It's an attractive piece of jewellery,' she defended. She was foolish to wear it constantly.

'Yes.' His brows gathered darkly as he stared at the brown liquid in the cup.

Silence pounded in the room. The strain of sitting immobile, hardly daring to breathe, maintaining the fragile pose of a near stranger had Joan's heart screaming with frustration.

'Brandt, why are you here?' she burst out suddenly, the drumbeat of her heart roaring in her ears.

The usage of his Christian name brought a quick gleam of satisfaction to the gaze that focused intently on the desperate look in her eyes. Then it slid rapidly to the bedroom door where Kay waited, an ear no doubt pressed to the keyhole.

'I want you to have dinner with me tonight.' Brandt's head was drawn back, a regal, leonine pose of alertness as his eyes missed none of the dismay etched in her features.

Her fingers closed over the arms of the rocker. She pushed herself violently out of the chair, leaving it rocking wildly behind her.

'No!' Her refusal was sharp and vigorous. The molten amber of her hair danced about her shoulders at the negative shake of her head.

Swiftly her feet carried her to the apartment window overlooking the street below. Concentrating her attention on the traffic, her sensitive radar still knew the instant Brandt rose to his feet. His steps were muffled by the carpet, but the vibrations relayed his approach behind her. She refused to turn her head even when her peripheral vision registered his profile, lean and sharply aquiline beside her.

A brown shirt of some clinging material moulded the broad shoulders with disturbing thoroughness. Brandt, too, stared into the street below them. His gaze lifted to the pale, winter blue sky.

'What I wouldn't give for a January blizzard!'

His swift glance at her was unexpected and it caught her covert study of him.

The thought of Brandt being marooned in her apartment twisted her already wounded heart. The consequences of such an event were too exquisitely painful to contemplate.

'Why would you wish for such a thing?' Coldly she rejected his veiled implication to stave off her own prayer for the same.

'Why?' Brandt echoed with bitter mockery. 'At least that once you exhibited some human reactions. I wasn't standing beside an emotionless creature.'

That biting comment was beyond calm acceptance. Emotionless! Every sinew registered his nearness. Every fibre cried out for his touch, however degrading the outcome when he would leave her to return to Angela. Retaliation for his sarcasm was demanded.

As she spun sharply around, her brown eyes flashing with avenging sparks, the open palm of her hand swung towards the infuriating curl of his mouth, taunting her lack of feeling. Inches from the tanned face, her movement was severely checked by an iron vice clamping itself around her wrist, unmindful of the hold that cut off circulation to her hand. Pride-born temper tilted her head back to let the force of her glaring anger be observed by his implacable face.

'You're the one who is despicable and disgusting, using people for your own satisfaction!' Joan accused bitterly. 'Always arrogantly forcing others to do what you want. Like a jungle beast, playing with people's feelings, dragging out their torture until they beg for mercy. Not me!'

Her wrist was twisted viciously to draw her nearer to the rock-hardness of his body while his other arm punishingly circled her waist to mould the rigid length of her more closely against him. It only took his touch to spark the kindled fires of her love. A quivering shudder of surrender raced through her even as her rounded velvet eyes pleaded with him for mercy, contradicting her declaration of an instant ago.

Dark blue eyes gleamed with wicked satisfaction as they read her fear. Then their attention was riveted on her parted, trembling lips. She formed the word 'no', but not a sound came from her throat and the sensuous line of his mouth moved hypnotically closer. Powerless to resist, Joan waited for his kiss.

Brutal possession accompanied the action, denying her breath. Crushed against him as she was, there was no opportunity to respond, but a gasping sigh slipped out when he angrily trailed his mouth over her neck. Her wrist was released, yet her arms were pinned against his chest, the thudding of his heart hammering against them. Blinded by the fury of his embrace, Joan was caught in a blizzard of emotions, lost to everything but his demands.

Suddenly his fingers dug into the silk of her robe, shoving her an arm's length away. Her lips throbbed from his bruising kiss, her head bowing weakly to shield the tormenting desire aching within. The curtain of her hair covered the scarlet shame warming her face.

'I'm not your employer any more, Joan,' Brandt declared huskily. 'Tell me to go or tell me to stay.'

'I can't let you stay,' she whispered.

'Why?' The demand was expelled with an angry breath. 'Don't you truly feel the same thing I do?' There was a sharp, vigorous shake of her shoulders. 'I'm a man and you're a woman. There are no other bonds between us, no business, nothing to make you obliged to obey me. If you don't want me, tell me to leave.'

'Brandt!' The despairing cry beseeched him not to make her acknowledge her love. 'Credit me with some pride and self-respect. I simply can't discount the way I've been raised, the values I've been brought up to believe in. I can't have an affair with you and still hold my head up. Leave. Go to Angela. And please leave me alone!'

'Angela? Who's talking about Angela?' he ground out harshly. 'She has no part in this discussion. This concerns you and me.'

'But ultimately she is involved.' Joan wrenched free of his hold, trying to put distance between them before she melted into his arms.

'Answer me one question,' Brandt demanded, 'Do you believe I love Angela?'

'Of course!' she cried out, hating the way he was deliberately torturing her with images of them. 'She's perfect. She's ideal.'

'But she doesn't run around in bare feet. She isn't a bull-headed, stubborn blonde who can't see two inches in front of her nose without her glasses!' His voice raised to a louder, more forceful volume.

Joan's mouth opened in disbelief. The look in the brilliant eyes studying her so calmly was sending her some message that she was certain she wasn't understanding correctly. She shook her head slightly.

'If you could see what's in front of your nose,' Brandt continued with slow deliberation, 'you could see that I love you.'

'Angela?' she breathed.

'Angela is a pretty china doll, just as you said. I've known her a long time. It didn't take me long to know she wasn't the type I wanted. I swear I haven't been alone with her, except for that luncheon date, since that weekend we were stranded.' His gaze narrowed. 'I love you, but do you care about me?' He hurried on before she had a chance to respond. 'I'll settle for affection right now. Anything for the time being. All I want is a chance to make you care as much as I do.'

'Care!' Joan laughed, happiness bubbling like a perpetual fountain from her heart. Weakly her hand passed over her forehead. 'I've loved you nearly every day that I've worked for you.'

In the next instant she was caught up in his arms. This time there was no effort to punish as he tenderly and gently kissed her again and again, touching her as if she were a fragile blossom. She cradled his rugged face in her hands.

'Brandt. is this real? Am I dreaming?' she murmured achingly.

'If it's a dream, I never intend to wake up unless it's with you in my arms,' Brandt vowed. 'If it hadn't been for that blizzard, I keep asking myself how long it would have taken me to see you as more than an attractive, competent secretary. When I took you on, I was afraid it wouldn't work. But you were always so formal. It was always business.'

'So were you,' Joan returned, slipping her arms around his neck.

'Then the electricity went out,' he smiled, brushing his mouth over her cheek. 'And it was so natural and right to sleep with you in my arms. It was nearly impossible to find that girl when the lights came back on.'

'She was hiding, afraid you would guess that she loved you.' Joan curled tighter in his arms, those strong arms that would always protect her and thrill her with their caress.

'Not afraid of losing her job?' Brandt mocked lightly.

'I gave it up, remember?' she whispered.

'I remember.' A feather light kiss brushed her lips before his head was drawn away. 'Kay!' He kept Joan in his arms, smiling at the slight flush in her cheeks. 'You can come out now.'

The bedroom door was opened and Kay hesitantly stepped out. Dark eyes glanced at Joan resting so contentedly in Brandt's arms, apprehension in their depths mixed with wary uncertainty.

'I think Joan would like you to be maid of honour at our wedding,' Brandt announced complacently.

At Joan's startled glance, his smile broadened, the radiant light in his blue eyes drawing a soft glow of happiness from hers. Her teeth bit into her trembling lip.

'Did I forget to ask you to be my wife?' he teased, unmindful of Kay's astonished look. 'That's the usual course of events when two people love each other, isn't it?'

'Yes.' Softly at first, then with a little cry of happiness, Joan repeated her acceptance. 'Yes, yes, it is.'

'Tonight we'll have dinner with my parents and tomorrow we'll drive to your home. Am I going too fast?' He tilted his head to the side, searching her face for a sign of uncertainty.

'Brandt—darling,' Joan laughed through her glittering tears. 'If anything, you aren't going fast enough!'

There was a sharp intake of breath at her words. Convulsively his arms tightened around her an instant before his mouth captured hers. Neither of them heard Kay, a tear of shared happiness slipping from her dark lashes, discreetly close the bedroom door behind her.

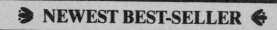

ATTRACTIVE, SPACE SAVING BOOK RACK

Display your most prized novels on this handsome and sturdy book rack. The hand-rubbed walnut finish will blend into your library decor with quiet elegance, providing a practical organizer for your favorite hard-or soft-covered books.

Only $9.95

Approximately 16" x 8" when assembled

Assembles in seconds!

To order, rush your name, address and zip code, along with a check or money order for $10.70* ($9.95 plus 75¢ postage and handling) payable to *Harlequin Reader Service*:

Harlequin Reader Service
Book Rack Offer
901 Fuhrmann Blvd.
P.O. Box 1325
Buffalo, NY 14269-1325

Offer not available in Canada.

BKR-1R

*New York residents add appropriate sales tax.

HARLEQUIN HISTORICAL

Explore love with Harlequin in the Middle
Ages, the Renaissance, in the Regency, the
Victorian and other eras.

Relive within these books the endless ages of
romance, set against authentic historical
backgrounds. Two new historical love stories
published each month.

Six exciting series for you every month... from Harlequin

Harlequin Romance
The series that started it all

Tender, captivating and heartwarming...
love stories that sweep you off to faraway places
and delight you with the magic of love.

◆

Harlequin Presents
Powerful contemporary love stories...as individual as the women who read them

The No. 1 romance series...
exciting love stories for you, the woman of today...
a rare blend of passion and dramatic realism.

◆

Harlequin Superromance®
It's more than romance... it's Harlequin Superromance

A sophisticated, contemporary romance-fiction
series, providing you with a longer,
more involving read...a richer mix of complex plots,
realism and adventure.

Harlequin
American Romance™
Harlequin celebrates the
American woman...

...by offering you romance stories written
about American women, by American women
for American women. This series offers you
contemporary romances uniquely North American
in flavor and appeal.

◆

Harlequin Temptation™
Passionate stories for
today's woman

An exciting series of sensual, mature stories of
love...dilemmas, choices, resolutions...
all contemporary issues dealt with in a true-to-life
fashion by some of your favorite authors.

◆

Harlequin Intrigue
Because romance can be quite
an adventure

Harlequin Intrigue, an innovative series that
blends the romance you expect...
with the unexpected. Each story has an added
element of intrigue that provides a new twist to
the Harlequin tradition of romance excellence.

Harlequin Books®

PROD-A-2

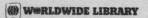